"Kiss me, Marcus."

I closed my eyes and responded to his kiss with an eagerness that made my whole body tingle. Then I pulled away hastily. The feel of him pressing against me through the thinness of my dress was unbearably pleasant, and terribly dangerous. Understanding, he laughed in a kindly way when he saw my embarrassment.

"One day, Salome, when I've made my fortune as a physician, we can be together like this always," Marcus whispered.

We clung to one another for a long while and murmured many things which I cannot put down, because they are the things men and women say when they are in love. I felt both a sense of wonderment at being loved by such a fine, honest man, and a sense of disappointment because I secretly believed his plans for our future were doomed to fail. But to have told him so would have broken his heart— and I loved him . . .

Pinnacle Books by John Jakes:

I, BARBARIAN
VEILS OF SALOME

JOHN JAKES
VEILS OF SALOME

(a new, revised and enlarged edition of the
original work previously written under the
pseudonym Jay Scotland)

PINNACLE BOOKS   NEW YORK CITY

VEILS OF SALOME

Copyright © 1962 by Jay Scotland
Copyright © 1976 by John Jakes

Pinnacle Books edition, published for the first time. Produced by Lyle Kenyon Engel

ISBN: 0-523-00972-0

First printing, October 1976

Cover illustration by Dean Cate

Printed in the United States of America

PINNACLE BOOKS, INC.
275 Madison Avenue
New York, N.Y. 10016

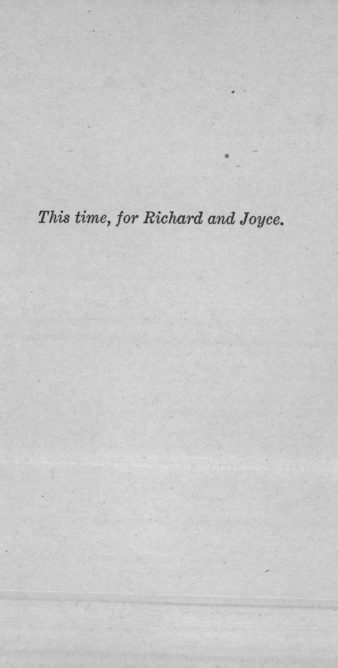

This time, for Richard and Joyce.

TABLE OF CONTENTS

VEILS OF SALOME

**Special Introduction
To the
Pinnacle Edition**

A lot of writers, I suspect, experience two different kinds of "ups and downs."

The first kind the writer knows nothing about. He sails along, convinced he's working at peak efficiency, only to discover after the manuscript's complete—or worse, published—that his judgment was as bad as his prose.

That's painful enough. But it doesn't begin to compare with the second, conscious kind, during which the "up" feeling seems a thing of the past, never to be achieved again; and the "down" is the way it is every day, and always will be.

Pseudonymous "Jay Scotland," whose origins were outlined in the Introduction to Pinnacle's edition of I, BARBARIAN, wrote THE VEILS OF SALOME during one of the "downs" described in the preceding paragraph. More accurately, the book was a way of fighting free of one of those exceedingly dark times.

Our family was living—reasonably well—in upstate New York. But for various reasons too tedious to go into here, I hit a stretch in which the writing I was doing not only didn't satisfy me, it disgusted me with its lack of quality. As the depression grew worse, the words-per-day grew fewer and fewer.

There are several solutions to such a problem. As one of my advertising friends used to say, "For starters, you get Rob Roys or religion." I never liked Rob Roys.

Since this is a story, not a tract, I won't digress into a metaphysical swamp. Suffice it to say that I've always held the belief (or hope) that there *is* some kind of order in the universe—as well as a universal promise of the possibility of change.

At the time this book was written, however, I wasn't—and have never been since—what you could call a devotee of "organized" religion. Cheerful and sociable as they may be, rituals such as the covered-dish suppers to which I was dragooned during my boyhood in the midwest have always struck me as pretty far removed from the real stuff of religion: questions of purpose, fallibility, forgiveness, love.

In fact, my first formal encounter with religion was almost catastrophic. I was inducted, if that's

2

the term, into a Baptist church when I was 12 or 13. Since Baptists practice immersion, one Sunday morning I was duly tugged backwards into the water of the baptistry by the reverend who lived in the apartment above ours. My feet popped off the baptistry floor and I began to *float*—after having been instructed to keep my feet firmly planted.

Panicky, I floundered, gulped, splashed. The desperate preacher at last restored me to the vertical. And though he never lost his smile, it seemed somewhat tight as he delivered the sermon with water dripping from his ears. I sat in a pew feeling more klutz than convert.

But in the depths of the bad period, I still went straight to a man, a pastor, whose tough profession it was to try to balance Biblical tenets and the day-to-day functioning of a church ("For God's sake who's bringing the macaroni salad??"). . . .

This good and wise man shut his office door for more hours than he could afford, and almost single-handedly lifted me out of the sloughs. He's still a pastor, and a fine one, so I won't include his name in case my scriptural interpretations should prove embarrassing to him. But we correspond from time to time, and he knows how deeply in his debt I am.

When things started to get a little better, I was not exactly transformed into a touring evangelist, mind you. But I began to get interested in the Bible as history and narrative literature. I enrolled, nights, as an auditor in a course at the excellent Colgate-Rochester Divinity School. A superb Biblical scholar surveyed the writings in the

3

Apocrypha—and Judean history between that covered in the Old and New Testaments.

It's a fascinating, tumultuous time, too often forgotten. And it's full of possibilities for the historical novelist. I've always wanted to do a book about one part of the period, and still hope to manage it one of these days.

When I, BARBARIAN seemed to be doing well enough to merit a follow-up, I was beginning to get my fingers back into contact with the typewriter keys, and the suggestion of a novel about the legendary Salome met with a good reception. You're holding the result.

I can't tell you how many charts I pored over, trying to get the various kings and emperors and governors straight. What also intrigued me was the side-by-side existence of the cultures of Rome and the Holy Land—a coexistence some Biblical novels ignore. I deliberately plotted this book so as to be able to suggest a few of the social, political, and religious differences between the two societies.

During the republication process this year, I was pleased to discover that SALOME's style didn't seem quite as florid as that of the original I, BARBARIAN. Some progress in Editorial Surgery As Conducted by the Author had evidently taken place between the original writing of both books. Not as many adjectives have been dumped from the first version of SALOME as was the case with the novel about Genghis Khan.

The book was also interesting to do from a technical standpoint. I didn't know whether a man could successfully write from a first-person

4

feminine viewpoint; I still don't. But it was a challenge to try.

Alas, when SALOME was first published, my pastoral mentor gave it only about a B+ (among his other good qualities, he was unfailingly—but never unkindly—honest). He liked the story but found the theology a little pat.

But it is, first and foremost, a *story*—so I hope you enjoy it on that basis; I'll always remember it as the work-therapy that brought a dark time to an end.

A few final notes of thanks:

To Andy Ettinger, Editor-in-Chief of Pinnacle Books, for helping SALOME come back to life.

To Lyle Kenyon Engel and Marla Ray for valuable assistance in arranging the reincarnation.

And especially to my wife Rachel. She has not only suffered (and I do mean *suffered)* the ups and downs that inevitably go with being married for twenty-five years to someone in a flaky profession, but she's helped me weather them. She's always there; and her support is not merely spiritual. Just today she finished a stint of editorial work on the revised manuscript of this novel.

JOHN JAKES

BOOK ONE

ROME

Chapter I

Omens

To begin it, I must tell of blue fire in the heavens above the Capitoline, and of demons that possessed me in the sultry dark.

All day, late summer heat had oppressed the seven hills. The stench of the great Tiber twisting in its fouled yellow course sickened even the hardiest of the male slaves in my father's house. When night fell, shrubs in the peristyle rustled in a hot, fitful wind. In the sky Jove Thunderer began to trace his messages with fingers of lightning. It was not so long ago, really, yet it seems

9

to be the lost age because of all I have lived through since.

My slave Gemma came to me that night while I was trying to sleep on the couch in my chamber. She begged to come close to me for protection.

The wick in the oil lamp blew and guttered. A crash from the front of the house set Gemma's teeth to chattering. "Mistress, devils are in the house. Jove Thunderer has loosed them."

"Nonsense," I said, though with little conviction. "It's only the wind knocking over some unimportant statue. Perhaps the little image of the dog my mother brought from the country a week ago."

Gemma's slim body trembled beneath her plain tunic. She crept back to the door. More frightened than ever, she looked out, then turned back.

"No, Mistress Salome. There are people in the atrium. Whatever broke has caused a great commotion."

"Then go see! But return quickly. I want my hair combed before I sleep. If I *can* sleep, with the air thick as wool."

She disappeared into the murmurous dark of the peristyle on swift naked feet. The lamp sputtered, nearly went out. From a corner I drew my best white palla and pulled it about my shoulders. Another peal of thunder shook the house. The sky above the peristyle glittered with the divine blue radiance of the god. The woolen shawl did no good. By turns I became chilled and feverish.

For a moment my own fear angered me. Why was I behaving like my slave? I was a grown woman, with mature breasts and white skin kept

10

soft by the milk of asses, while Gemma was but a child of fourteen, a whole year younger than I. It was my duty to show my slave she had nothing to fear from an ordinary summer storm. Was I not the sole child of my father, young mistress of his sprawling house? Was I not three years beyond marriageable age and fit to bear a son or daughter?

All of that was true. But the year would not leave me. The heat of the night chilled and burned me by turns. Perhaps there was good reason for fear. Of late, rumors had flown in the city that the gods of Imperial Rome were growing angry over the worship of foreign deities, such as those a certain unspeakable member of our household chose to venerate. Too long, it was said, Jove Thunderer had tolerated the casual indifference of many Roman citizens. Some said his vengeance would be fearful.

By day I might not have even thought of such tales. Educated Roman citizens said that the gods were merely oversized mortals. Like street vendors, they could be bribed. I believed it too, for if I was not exactly a Roman citizen by birth—my father being descended from the fierce Idumaean kings—I had certainly been well educated, and wanted for nothing. And yet I cringed on my couch when Jove Thunderer smote the sky that night.

Why was Gemma gone so long? Impatiently I crossed to the doorway. The boughs in the peristyle whipped in the wind. To the right, in the direction of the atrium, I saw the flicker of torches. Clearly there was alarm in our household, and I determined to find out what caused it.

11

Gathering my shawl about me and picking up the hem of my stola, I took a step into the dark.

A hideous white face leaped up before me in a burst of lightning.

"Gemma!" I fell back, gasping. "Don't come creeping through the dark that way."

"Creeping, Mistress? Not creeping—running for my life! Let us go inside at once. This is an evil night."

I tried to push past her into the howling wind. "No! I want to see—"

Tears sprang to the corners of her dark eyes. She clutched my arms in a manner unbefitting a slave, but there was such terror on her face that I could not speak angrily.

"You don't wish to see what I have seen, Mistress. There is a dead man lying at the gate—"

"May the sacred virgins protect us! Who!"

"I don't know, Mistress. A cart-man, Thoth said—"

At the mention of the Alexandrine slave, my flesh crawled, but I said nothing as Gemma rushed on.

"He was bringing his load of cabbages into the city by night because the law forbids carts by day. It's an evil law that sends a man abroad on such a night."

"The law of Tiberius Claudius Nero is just," I said, echoing a phrase which had gained currency when the aging Emperor had imposed the peace of Rome upon the vast empire fifteen years earlier, in the year of his ascension and my birth. Still, I gained little comfort from the words.

When I was again seated on the couch in my

room, Gemma rested her head against my knee. Her thin shoulders shook.

"But it's still an evil law, Mistress," she said suddenly, "though I may be whipped for daring to say such a thing. The ox hauling the cart went wild at the thunder and lightning. The cart-man fell under the iron wheels and was trampled. In the open door I saw his head running with blood. But his eyes were still open. And white like—"

"Hold your tongue, girl!"

Gemma obeyed. She lowered her head. But her eyes remained fixed in space, round and frightened. I think she knew I would ask to hear more. Terror had seized me. It was more than fear of the storm and Jove Thunderer. It sprang from knowing that a dark and dreadful time had been long due to fall upon our house—a house of coldness and anger. A house where whispering and rancor had long ago replaced kindly discourse and love.

"Tell me the rest, Gemma. Perhaps then we can sleep."

"In the alcove off the atrium, the ceremonial bust of your father's father, the great King Herod who once ruled all of the Jewish lands beyond the sea—"

She bit her lip, unable to continue.

I stroked her hair, black and lustrous as mine. "Continue, Gemma. I am the daughter of this household, and venerate the gods every morning with offerings. Nothing can hurt you when you're with me," I finished emptily.

After a moment she said, "The wind smashed the wax bust of Herod the Great."

13

For a long moment I didn't fully grasp the significance of this omen.

"That's impossible, Gemma—"

"No, Mistress. I saw it scattered in a hundred pieces."

Suddenly, terror-stricken, I clasped my arms tight around her shoulders and swayed from side to side, feeling hot salt tears on my cheeks. In an instant I had become the frightened child and Gemma the protectress.

"What is to become of us, Gemma—of *this house?* It's an evil place. All of us smile like play actors, only pretending to be polite and civil. I've never said this, Gemma, but I hate this house. There's nothing here but a hunger for money. It drives my father half out of his mind worrying over his racing company. It makes my mother fawn over and throw herself at the wives of wealthy senators, who will never accept her for anything more than a foreign woman whose husband bought his citizenship with cash, not with true Roman blood."

"But at least there's Marcus. That should be some comfort."

"It would be if my mother would let me marry him."

"Then you could leave this house, and take me with you!"

With a sigh I shook my head. "It's a dream, Gemma. Marry a freedman? Especially one holding the lowly office of physician? Unless my mother turns into another person and the dawn becomes the dark, it's not likely. The only reason I'm not in the marriage bed of some young knight already is because my father and mother are foreigners. The wealthy families breed only with their own kind."

A crafty look crossed Gemma's face. "We could run away together—"

"And what would we live on? My splendid wealth? I have none of my own. And we'd both be murdered if the legions of Tiberius caught us. You for running away, me for helping you."

Alas, I had only succeeded in talking Gemma into more tears. She clutched at me, wailing. "Then what's to become of us?"

"Perhaps Jove Thunderer will solve our problems, and—and end our lives this very night."

Horrified, she stared at me. But suddenly I could no longer control the strange feelings. I burst out with sobbing nearly as wild as hers.

"I'm not as strong as I pretend, Gemma. I'm just as frightened as you. I'm frightened by a dead man on our doorstep and the statue of my grandfather destroyed, I'm frightened because my mother and father hate each other. And worst of all because I've found the one thing I want most—Marcus. I can't have him because he was once a slave."

That night, the night in which so many strands that were to become part of the fabric of my life were first woven into the pattern, Gemma and I must have sounded like a pair of wailing cats, of the kind Thoth the Alexandrine had brought with him when he was purchased for our household. Someone gazing upon us huddled together might have called it a comic scene. Yet it was not comedy but the beginning of an evil time.

Finally, driven to exhaustion by my own crying, I fell into a restless sleep. Gemma curled up

15

at the foot of the hard wooden couch my father considered necessary for proper development of the bones. I lay there in agony sickened by heat, blinded by frequent bursts of lightning above the peristyle. My linen nightdress twisted about my hips in damp folds as I rolled from side to side, palms against my eyelids, trying to hide from a formless horror which seemed to hover close.

The lamp had gone out long ago. The wind howled. Distant voices cried in the street. And then devils of nightmare came to possess me. They foretold with fearful accuracy what my life would be from this night forward!

The first dream was that of a head running scarlet with blood.

At first I thought it was the head of the unfortunate cart-man. It hovered near me, the eyes bright as a hawk's. I struggled to escape, turning to run through limitless darkness. It came floating after me, its hoary locks streaming blood. Then it began to recede. Its mouth opened. A mournful sound came from it, sad and anguished all at once.

But I had escaped. I turned away from it—

And fell screaming through an abyss into the churning waves of the Mare Nostrum.

The great sea heaved and foamed in the thunder of a raging storm. Upon the water I saw a mighty trireme buffeted. The ship was helpless in the grip of the elements. I seemed to be floating near the pitching vessel, close enough to make out the faces of the travelers sprawled on the deck. Even the women had male heads.

The heads were fat, saffron colored, the eyelids puffed and ugly, the skulls gleaming with oil.

Thoth the Alexandrine, worshipper of Isis, stroking his cat with the blue-green eyes. . . .

Then another strange thing occurred. My eyes opened—or so I thought. While I could not see with perfect clarity, I could make out the doorway to the peristyle. Beyond, the faint gray light dawn glimmered. It revealed a squat figure standing there watching me.

Watching with liquid brown eyes while oiled cheeks swelled in silent mirth.

I flung myself over on the couch, burying my head in my arms to shut out that malignant face. I let the nightmare claim me again—if the vision of Thoth's face had indeed been reality.

In the rest of the dream I saw the great temple of the Thunderer on the Capitoline Hill struck by lightning bolts that smoked and hissed. I saw the mammoth marble statue of the god himself topple from its pedestal, falling forward to crush me. Another lightning bolt smote the carven chest. It flew apart. I could not run fast enough to escape. A thousand pieces of marble rained down, burying me.

Chapter II

House of Enemies

"Mistress! Mistress Salome, wake up! It's already past the second hour."

Slowly I opened my eyes. With a start I sat upright. Feeling a chill, I looked down. My breasts, of which I was so foolishly proud upon their maturing, were bare.

Gemma pointed to the shreds of the night dress at my waist. "You've torn your gown, Mistress."

"In a bad dream," I said, rising and trying to shake off the memory of the nightmare. I heard a busy clatter from across the peristyle. "What's that racket at this time of the day? Is the whole household awake?"

"Oh, yes, and it's most exciting." Gemma's eyes were round. "A courier arrived, bearing tablets for your father from his half-brother."

"Which one?" I asked crossly. There were two. Phillip the Tetrarch had been fathered by King Herod and Cleopatra of Jerusalem. With fair Malthrace he had begotten Herod Antipas. My own father had been sired by Herod and a woman named Miramne.

I reached for my morning stola, fastening it over my shoulders, and drew on a bridle crusted with pearls which my father had given me for my twelfth birthday.

"Ah, Gemma, you've no idea what a trial it is to come from a race of kings. The endless squabbling! Whose mother was the most beautiful. Which of the three half-brothers suffered most when Herod the Great refused to name any of them king of the land of the Jews. Arguments— always arguments."

Gemma laughed as I seated myself on a stool. She began to untangle my hair with a horn comb. "At least you can smile about things this morning."

"But who did the tablets come from?"

"Antipas, the tetrarch of—I don't remember."

"Galilee and Perea, wherever they may be. I've heard my father say Phillip the Tetrarch is old and feeble, hardly a ruler at all. He controls Trachonitis and Iturea, somewhere near a river called Jordan. Don't ask me anymore because I don't know any more."

"Still, such an arrival is an exciting way to be-

19

gin the day, don't you think?" Gemma plied the comb expertly, binding my hair with carved ivory pins. "I don't feel as bad as I did last night. The storm has passed. Everything is bright again. Even if the statue of Jove Thunderer did tumble—"

"The statue on the Capitoline?"

"Yes. One of the tradesmen told Thoth. The statue broke to pieces."

I shivered. "Gemma, did you sleep beside me during the night?"

"Most of the night, Mistress. Why?"

"I had terrible visions. One of them concerned the statue. And once I think I woke up. I thought I saw the Alexandrine standing in the doorway, watching me. Almost as though he wanted— Gemma, do you understand my meaning?"

Streaks of pink crept into Gemma's cheeks. "Mistress Salome, Thoth is a eunuch. Even if the Egyptian god of magic from whom he got his name sat on his shoulder to help him, he would still be unable—" Gemma clapped her hands over her mouth and laughed. "What a funny dream. The eunuch? Oh, Mistress, forgive my laughing—"

"I certainly won't. There's nothing amusing about the Alexandrine." I leaned down to pick up the torn dress when I noticed strange stains on the fabric.

"Gemma—look! It's stained with some sort of oil."

"How odd."

Shuddering, I flung the garment away.

"Whose hands are oiled in this house, Gemma?"

20

"Mistress, he wouldn't dare touch you in your sleep, no matter what desires torture him."

"Wouldn't he? He's an evil man, Gemma. He purrs and whispers like that beastly cat of his. And he panders to every foolish desire my mother has." Fear overcame me again as I gazed upon the spotted gown. I dreaded Thoth more than ever now. Yet my dread was based solely upon a dream—the oil might have been spilled when I lit the lamp at nightfall.

Gemma, however, was no longer in a mood to listen to my fears.

"Please, Mistress, you'd better go at once to the dining chamber. Your parents have nearly finished the morning meal. Your mother will have me beaten if I'm responsible for your being late. She's very excited over the prospect of a visit from Herod Antipas."

"A visit!" I exclaimed, slipping into my sandals. "You said nothing about a visit—"

"It was mentioned in the tablets. Thoth told me," Gemma replied as we walked across the peristyle.

"That swollen fox knows entirely too much for the good of this household."

My confidence was bolstered by the morning light falling into the open court. I breathed deeply, pleased by the feel of my own body beneath the stola. I knew I was a woman and would one day claim a woman's birthright of love. Perhaps from Marcus Catullus if the gods were kind. At least, I would make a better mother than mine had been to me.

We passed the bustling scullery where the slaves were at work and reached the dining hall.

21

As was custom, my mother Herodias and my father Herod Phillip were reclining on masonry benches built about the sides of the room. The remains of the morning meal littered the table between them. My mother sat up quickly as a cat when I entered. My father continued to be absorbed in a piece of parchment which, from its seals, I recognized as one of an endless stream of communications from the racing stables of the Blue faction.

My mother was a handsome woman. She had dark hair, a prominent nose, and olive skin. Her bright, sloping eyes were rimmed with kohl. She had not lost her figure bearing me. In fact she looked extremely youthful, and had large breasts, about which I had heard more than one of our slaves make a bawdy joke. Bitter fountains they called them, those breasts.

I took my place on my own bench. My mother dipped a last piece of bread into the breakfast wine and regarded me with displeasure.

"One would think you the daughter of a nobleman, Salome, rather than the child of a plain man of commerce. We can hardly be called a proper Roman family if word gets about that we're lazy and don't rise at dawn."

My father continued frowning at his parchment. I wanted to retort sharply that I preferred the confines of my room to the company of my parents, but I held my tongue until I was calm enough to say.

"I ask your pardon, Mother. The storm and all the noise last night kept me awake."

My mother shuddered. "Some plebian run over in the street. I hope someone's hauled off the

22

corpse by now, or we'll have a filthy smell in the house."

At this point my father looked up. His eyes were dark. "By all means send one of the slaves to cart him off, Herodias. Two of the chief directors of the Blues will be calling at the sixth hour. There's a possibility I may be granted additional stock."

"How can you think about that damnable racing company when we have an important visitor coming to see us in a few weeks?" she blazed back. "There are dozens of things to be done: an apartment to be decorated for him—"

"For my half-brother?" Herod Philip was startled. "May I ask why it's necessary to go to such trouble?"

Herodias snatched up the bound wooden tablets lying on the table. She opened them and touched a long nail to the Greek letters inscribed in the mixture of blacking and wax with which the wood was coated.

"Didn't you bother to read this message?"

My father sighed, put down his parchment, and straightened himself to a sitting position. His toga with its thin purple stripe fell down over his spindly legs. He had no doubt been a handsome man in his youth, but he had long ago resigned himself to being a man of small consequence in the world of commerce, and it showed. He was doomed to wear the thin stripe forever, rather than the wider one of the nobly born.

Irritated, he stared at my mother for several moments. Then he uttered another long sigh. He had long since lost any semblance of spirit, and now contented himself with plodding pursuit of his own small goals. For a moment I felt ashamed, thinking about him so coldly. Yet in all my life I could remember only a very few times when he had displayed any affection toward me. Only one thing did he love.

"Herodias," he complained, "are you aware of the stakes in the forthcoming chariot race?"

"I have absolutely no interest in your company and you know it."

"That's a pity. My shares in the company provide us with the luxury in which we live."

She laughed. *"Luxury?* It may seem luxury to a freedman like that physician over whom Salome makes calf-eyes. It should hardly seem so to you, a man with the blood of kings in his veins."

"Who would want to be king of those god-forsaken provinces on the other side of the world?"

"Obviously your brother Herod Antipas does. He's coming to Rome to see the Emperor. What other purpose could he have but to sue again for the kingship Herod the Great thought none of his sons worthy of holding?"

"Then he'll be disappointed," my father said. "Tiberius has gone back to Capri."

My mother looked upset. "When?"

"A week ago. He spends more time on that island than he does in Rome. People say he isn't even interested in the Empire anymore. He leaves everything to the control of that rogue Sejanus who heads the Praetorians." A mildly mocking smile. "On the other hand if Tiberius has indeed gone senile as people say, perhaps Antipas will be able to persuade him to give him the crown of the Herods after all."

24

"I can't see what you find so contemptible about a kingship. Think of the wealth! The connections of the Imperial Court. But then you're not interested in such things, are you? You never have been—not in all the years since we've been married. The prize has been there, if only you were strong enough to take it. But all you care about is that beastly gang of ruffians in the Blues—"

"Woman, I earn my livelihood working with those men. I'll not have them slandered!"

For one wild moment I wished that he would strike my mother in the face. Instead, he uttered another sigh, blinked, and began tapping the parchment against his palm.

"Herodias, let me reiterate a few facts. Unless the Blue racing company wins heavily at the next games, the losses we've suffered of late at the provincial little circuses will begin to hurt. There'll be fewer coins in the family purse. What happens when the Blues next compete in the Circus Maximus has a very real bearing on our welfare. And this very note contains very bad news. Our Centenarius has pulled a leg muscle."

"You can kill the horse for all I care!" my mother cried.

My father thought she was joking. "Kill a prize Libyan stallion that's won more than a hundred races? Why don't we kill Castor, our champion charioteer, too, and be done with it? Then we could guarantee bankruptcy."

"If you had the ambition of Antipas, you'd forget your damned horses and seek the crown of Judea."

25

"I've told you, woman, I have no ambition to be king."

"And that's why you're not half the man your brother is!"

At this my father jumped up, gathered his toga about him and stalked toward the door. There, however, he stopped to glance at me. His face softened a little. I felt a sudden sorrow for the way he was constantly demeaned by my mother. He said:

"Salome, I regret you have to listen to such talk. I often wish you had been born a male child. Then I could leave my stock in the Blues to you when I die, and you'd come to understand why I find only a sense of accomplishment in racing. As it is—" He flung my mother a glance of disgust. "You'll no doubt be drawn into your mother's glorious plans for entertaining Antipas. But don't forget this, either of you. Unless Castor drives the Libyan to win, we'll be feeding our guest gruel and precious little else."

So saying, he left the chamber. My mother hurried to my side.

"Eat, child, while I tell you about my plans."

I glanced at the breakfast raisins and olives sprinkled with salt.

"I'm not hungry."

"But you don't want to look all skin-and-bones when you dance for Antipas."

"I'm hardly all skin and bones now. Besides, I've only taken training in dancing to give me something to do. I wasn't entitled to go to the grammar school like the boys."

She bent close to me, her painted lips widening in a smile that was almost crafty.

"Still, you're a lovely young woman. Your dancing will bring pleasure to our visitor. Antipas is an important man. His star may very well be rising at the court of Tiberius."

"Perhaps you would have done better to have married him, Mistress."

I whirled. There stood the fat Alexandrine. It was he who had spoken.

His naked skull gleamed with oil, and his evil cat perched on his shoulder with its tail twined around his neck.

"Is it your habit to eavesdrop, Thoth?" I said.

"No, my lady," he replied in his low, bland voice. I could not make out his eyes, so deeply sunken in fat were they, but I knew he was studying me. People said strange things happened to the brains of men made eunuchs by the knife, and I could well believe it of this sly, secretive creature.

But my mother was all smiles. She patted his jeweled hand affectionately.

"Don't be sharp with Thoth, Salome. He is wise in ways Romans can't understand. When he says Antipas would have made an ideal husband, he only speaks the truth."

"No! He twists words to cater to your desires, Mother. Everyone has ambitions. Everyone wants things they can't have. But I'm old enough to know that people only make themselves miserable pretending some things are attainable."

"All things are possible if there is sufficient will," Thoth murmured.

"I won't listen to such talk against my father!"

"Why do you defend him, Salome?" said my mother. "He only loves his company. Not you, not

27

me, not this house nor his status—only those cursed animals and his companions at the stable."

"But he's your husband and my father! We owe him respect. I'll not hear his name dragged through the dirt."

Thoth touched my arm. "One moment, my lady."

"Keep your filthy hands off me!"

"A thousand apologies." the Eunuch withdrew his hand. "But permit me to overstep myself with a bit of advice. Should you talk too freely about affairs which don't concern you, you would certainly bring great unhappiness into this house. As a loyal servant I would not wish to see that happen."

"What affairs? If you mean this senseless, indecent chatter about my mother and Antipas, then it's you who ought to watch your tongue!"

Instead of taking the rebuke as an ordinary slave would have done, Thoth smiled, the corners of his moist lips curling upward.

"I believe I failed to make myself clear, Mistress. Not only would you bring great unhappiness into this house, but you might bring it down on your own head as well."

"Mother—will you allow a slave to stand here and threaten me?"

A swift glance flew from my mother to Thoth. Then she swung her gaze to me. I had never seen her look more cold, though her brightly stained lips smiled.

"Heed Thoth, Salome. He is a wise person."

With a cry I rushed from the room, not knowing exactly what Thoth had meant by his words, but knowing unmistakably that there was menace in his warning. When I passed the dining chamber a little later, hunting Gemma so that we might wander in the markets, the eunuch and my mother were still whispering together. I hurried on. I believed the omens had been correct. Though I did not know how it would come to pass, I believed that evil days would soon fall upon our house.

Chapter III

Fortunes of the Blues

A full week passed before I was able to decide whether I should try to counter the threat posed by the obvious conniving of my mother and Thoth the Alexandrine.

It was a week of torment and indecision. My father was gone from the house most of the time, being occupied at the Blue stables with the training of the charioteer and the team for the great race.

This gave me long hours in which to ponder whether I would be betraying my mother if I did what I wanted to do.

30

Yet her support of Thoth had been unmistakable. And the rush of activity in our household—the sweeping, the cleaning, the daubing of fresh crimsons and yellows upon the walls of the upper sleeping rooms reserved for our forthcoming guest—gave me reason to believe that Herodias considered Herod Antipas no ordinary visitor.

It was almost as though my mother were making ready for a lover, so excited and high-strung did she become. This realization at last forced my decision to speak to my father.

Although in my own heart I could find little real love for him—it saddened me to think this, and made me wonder whether I was a cold person—I did believe I owed him filial respect. Yet I still might not have gone to the stables of the Blues, but for the fact that I had not seen Marcus Catullus for several weeks.

So one morning I called for my litter and set out, telling myself I could always change my mind at the last moment if I decided that my father would think me a suspicious little fool.

The streets of Rome were thronged that day. But the crowd seemed small compared to the throng of onlookers who had gone to the countryside to watch Castor train his team. My slaves had to beat a path through a mob at the edge of the dirt practice track. The track had been laid out at the base of a low hill on the outskirts of the city. High on the hill bulked the rambling barracks and stables maintained by the Blue corporation. Knots of people sat on the hillside for a better view, and each had a bit of blue cloth or a scarf to denote partisanship for my father's company.

There was a pounding of hooves in a cloud of dust far down the track as I climbed from the litter. The scene made me understand why the four great racing companies—the Reds, Greens, Whites, and Blues—were among the biggest business enterprises in the Imperial dominion. First of all, they employed hundreds of men, including trainers and breakers of the Sicilian, Iberian, and Libyan horses, as well as charioteers' assistants, men whose task it was to grease the chariot wheels, others responsible for shining the orange chariot fittings, grooms and saddlers and dozens more whose work I did not begin to understand.

Moreover, the chariot companies drew together some of the wealthiest of Rome's business community, along with shareholders like my father who held less exalted rank. I saw a group of directors, my father among them, standing at the track's perimeter and walked toward them.

Just then, the light wooden practice chariot became visible in the dust. A cry of excitement rose from the throats of slaves and spectators. Castor the charioteer had brought the team around the far turn too sharply. The chariot threatened to tip. The Libyan stallion had been put on traces on the left side, as was customary, and he was straining and pulling under the flick of Castor's whip to wrench the other three horses to the left, exactly as though he were rounding the spine in the Circus Maximus.

The chariot righted with a jolt and surged forward. A cheer went up. Now the combination of a swift Sicilian stallion on the right side and the two Iberians yoked in the center showed its worth. Castor drove the team past my father's group in a burst of speed that brought loud applause. Then Castor slowed, turned, and came rolling back.

The directors surged forward. His young body gleaming with sweat and his teeth flashing in the sun, Castor took off his leather cap. He unwound the traces from his waist while slaves wiped his body with sponges and passed him a cup of wine.

Drawing near the chariot, I caught my father's eye. He signaled that he would come to my side in a moment.

Suddenly I caught my breath. On the far side of the chariot, I saw a strongly-chiseled, familiar face.

His powerful frame was clad in a simple tunic. His large, but surprisingly supple hands probed and squeezed the charioteer's muscles as he examined Castor after the strenuous run and near-upset. An examination was customary after a strenuous period.

Marcus saw me coming, grinned and waved. I responded in kind, unconcerned by shocked whispers of astonishment among the crowd. I was recognized as the daughter of Herod Philip. To display public affection for a freedman was unthinkable. But my love for Marcus had been unthinkable from the first day I chanced upon him as he worked over a hoof in the dim, hay-fragrant stables, awkward and shy when I introduced myself, but soon smiling that magical smile which forever bewitched me. I would love him until the day of my death, even though custom and class forbade it.

"I'm going to bet every denarius you can

scrape up, Vexus," I heard my father exclaim to one of the directors. "I'll either win a small fortune on Castor or lose everything except the walls of my house. But I won't suffer another season of being bled dry by losses in the provinces, that I warrant you."

"You won't be alone if you lose," one of the directors responded. "There isn't a man here who isn't sinking everything on the Centenarius."

"But our stock won't be worth air if we lose," another grumbled.

"Lose? With Castor driving? Impossible!" My father laughed, and walked toward me. His cheeks were flushed with excitement. He frowned as he took my arm and directed me through the crowd.

"Salome, this hurly-burly is no place for you."

"I wanted to see the team run. I know how important this race is."

His eyes clouded. "Do you? I wonder. Your mother fills you with so many foolish dreams— dreams even the gods couldn't bring to pass."

"I've said a prayer at the household shrine every day for a week, Father. I'll make offering in your behalf on the day of the race."

"That's certainly a strange change in attitude," he said, though without malice. "We've seen so little of one another the past year or so, I hardly blame you for taking your mother's part."

"That's what I came to talk about, Father. Walk with me to the poplar grove, where we can speak privately."

"If this is another of your pleas for me to sanction your marriage to our young physician—"

34

"No, Father. I understand why that's impossible."

"You understand it, but do you accept it?"

I faced him at the edge of the sunlit grove. "Yes."

"On that point, at least, your mother and I stand united. No sensible father would let his daughter marry beneath her. Of course," he added, with an understanding smile that seemed foreign to his nature, "if you want to come here discretely and walk with Marcus and hold his hand—why, I suppose every girl is entitled to a fling. Provided you don't get yourself into trouble. Now, what was it you wanted? I'm very busy. We're running another trial lap as soon as Castor's rested."

"Father—" The words came hard. "I felt I needed to warn you about my mother."

His eyes grew bitter. "About what? Nothing she does could surprise me any longer."

"She's conniving with Thoth—"

"For what purpose?"

"I'm not sure. But they have their heads together morning and night. All they talk about is how important it is to make a good impression on Antipas when he arrives."

"Are you afraid your mother will make a fool of herself by putting on some ostentatious display?"

I stopped. How could I tell him that I feared they plotted his betrayal? What sort of betrayal? I did not know.

"It's difficult for me to explain clearly, father. There's something wrong in the house. Terribly wrong. I—I don't want to see you hurt."

Impatiently he glanced restlessly to the track. "I'm hardened to hurt, Salome. Your mother has taught me well."

Just then, an anxious murmur rose from the crowd of directors near the chariot. I noticed Marcus still examining Castor. My father started away from the poplar grove, his brows drawn together in concern.

"Daughter, I must be off."

I seized his arm. "No, you must listen! You must believe me when I tell you Mother and Thoth are plotting something."

"But you don't know what."

I shook my head. "No."

"Salome, I'm a busy man. I'm grateful for your interest, but I can't be concerned with groundless suspicions. Not with race day drawing so close. I suggest you return to the city immediately. I'm likely to be occupied here until well after dark."

"Father! Please wait. You must believe what I'm trying to tell—"

It was useless. He was gone, running to see why the directors were clustered about their charioteer. I was angered and hurt by his rebuff. True, I had no evidence to support my suspicions. But even if I'd had such evidence I doubted he would have taken time to listen. The race was all that mattered. It was as though a water clock had measured out the precise fraction of time he was willing to spend with me.

Feeling miserable, I wandered out to the track while one of my litter bearers held a parasol over my head. I longed to talk to Marcus, but he was deep in animated talk with the directors. The conversation continued while Castor mounted the chariot and went racing around the track twice more.

When the practice laps were finished, Marcus and the directors surrounded the chariot again. All were asking questions of Castor, who had a sickly look on his face. The charioteer knelt down and wagged his head from side to side as though dizzy. Marcus bent over him. I moved forward to listen.

"Are you still bothered with the same complaint?" Marcus asked.

Castor nodded. "My head feels like I've swallowed ten jugs of wine."

Expertly Marcus conducted another examination of the young charioteer, probing here, poking there, in the manner of the learned Greek physicians who lectured upon their art every morning in the Temple of Peace in the city. When Marcus finished his examination, he frowned.

"Perhaps the jolt when the chariot almost spilled jarred you, Castor."

"I felt bad long before that," Castor said.

Swinging around, Marcus faced the directors. "Then I can only conclude you gentlemen have been working our prize charioteer too hard. I'm as interested in winning the race as you. But we're certain to lose unless Castor is allowed some rest between workouts. Too much training can wear him down. So can sheer worry."

Thereupon Marcus instructed Castor to leave the track for two days, drinking and eating nothing but wine, water, and lettuce. He was to bathe once a day at the frigidarium of the public baths. Finally Marcus spoke again to the directors.

37

"In your zeal to enter a winning team, don't forget the man is as important as the horses."

"And don't you get impertinent," someone muttered. "After all, it wasn't so long ago that you were a slave physician for our rivals the Greens, until your owner freed you."

Anger kindled in Marcus' eyes. "But now I'm a freedman, sir. If you don't want my professional opinion—dismiss me. I know I can find work elsewhere."

"Now, now, Marcus," my father said. "We trust your judgment. It's just that we're all fretting about the race. Only Castor can handle the Libyan."

"Please, masters," a voice exclaimed. "If Castor is ailing, let me take his place."

Through the crowd pressed a pale youth with rather large eyes. His upper arms were like thick ropes. I had seen him driving practice teams before. He stood before my father, smiling in a fawning way.

"I've waited for a chance like this for years, Masters," he said.

My father clapped him on the shoulder.

"Yes, Olipor, we know you're faithful. But it's no reflection on your skills when I say we can't afford to have anyone but Castor driving for us. I wouldn't count on driving. We'll follow the advice of the physician and let Castor rest more frequently."

The directors murmured assent. My father added, "Your time will come, Olipor, your time will come." He turned his back and fell into conversation while the disappointed Olipor slunk off, head down.

The practice runs were finished for the day. A handler mounted the chariot and started the team around the track at a trot to exercise them. Castor's assistants rushed him up the hill to the barracks buildings so he could rest.

Marcus had at last seen his chance to break away from the group. As always, when I saw him standing tall and tanned, I felt an excitement almost beyond bearing. Like a silly child, I waited for his smile. It did not appear. He took my arm and practically dragged me toward the poplar grove. His expression was black as a storm.

Chapter IV

Marcus and Caligula

"Always they throw it in my face!" he growled. *"You're a freedman but you're still a slave to us.* If it weren't for the possibility that they'd use their influence against me, I'd smash their foppish faces for them."

"That's not fair, Marcus. Only one of the directors spoke out of turn."

As we reached the fringes of the grove, Marcus at last managed to smile.

"Yes, you're right, as usual. I know they pay me handsomely, but when they remind me of what I was, I detest them."

"Don't forget, Marcus, the law says your former owner could take you back into slavery as easily as he set you free." I touched his arm, feeling a thrill in my fingertips. "I couldn't bear that."

"Well, it's only because of you that I keep my peace," he replied. He cupped one hand beneath my chin raising my face toward his. "I'm a very bad son, because I forget my parents living on their farm up in the country. I forget that reprisals could be taken against them too, since our owner set our whole family free at one time. I'm a very bad son because I think less of them than I do of you."

"I'm glad. Kiss me, Marcus."

Merriment sparkled in his gaze. "Your father would have me whipped if he sees me do it."

"Will that stop you?"

"Do you suppose so?" Laughing, he pulled me into his arms.

The smell of him, the male smell mingled with the scent of leather and wool of his clothing welled up around me. I closed my eyes and responded to his kiss with an eagerness that made my whole body tingle.

Then I pulled away hastily. The feel of him pressing against me through the thinness of my stola was unbearably pleasant, and terribly dangerous. Understanding, he laughed in a kindly way when he saw my embarrassment. Then he took my hand and led me to a bench at the fringe of the grove.

Out of sight of the spectators near the track, I leaned my head on his shoulder. Sunlight fell through the poplar leaves and warmed us. A finch warbled overhead. There seemed no time nor

41

space, no Rome, no race, no dark secrets in my house—only peace.

"One day, Salome, when I've made my fortune as a physician, we can be together like this always."

"And what am I supposed to do in the meantime?" I teased. "Content myself with a cold pallet when the winter wind blows out of Gaul?"

"Don't jest. I hate the idea of waiting. But we must. We can't marry in Rome. I'll never grow rich as a doctor here where there are hundreds of Greek and slave physicians available any hour of the day or night. It's true I get good wages from the Blues, but not the kind I need to marry you. In a foreign land—perhaps Germania or even those islands beyond, where they mine tin—my services would command a premium price. Does it matter that we don't live in Rome if it means we can be together as man and wife?"

"Nothing matters, darling, if that's what's necessary."

"But I wonder sometimes," he said pensively, "whether you will wait for me."

"Of course I will."

"Your mother wants you to marry—"

"Some pomaded fish who belongs to a senatorial family. The chance of that happening is about as great as the chance of the Libyan sprouting wings and winning the race by flying. I'm a citizen, Marcus, but I'm still a foreigner."

"But I'm only a freed slave—"

"Hush." I laid my fingers across his mouth. "Why doubt me so? I've told you I love you. I'd love you if you still belonged to your former owner. Even if you were a savage from Gaul with a beard to your knees."

"Salome, I praise the gods for bringing you into my sight. You're beautiful. Do you know how beautiful? Let me tell you—"

I laughed and called him flatterer and kissed him passionately. We clung to one another for a long while, there in our sunlit seclusion. We murmured many things which I cannot put down, because they are the things men and women say when they are in love, and are for no one else's ears. I felt both a sense of wonderment at being loved by such a fine, honest man, and a sense of disappointment because I secretly believed his plans for our future were doomed to fail. But to have told him so would have broken his heart.

Finally, as the shadows began to lengthen in the grove and the air grew cool, he drew away and reached for the pouch at his waist in which he usually kept his little pots of ointment and a few surgical tools.

"Marcus, you look like a guilty schoolboy. Why?"

"I've bought you something. I argued price for nearly an hour with the craftiest merchant in all Rome. I've been planning a pretty little speech when I presented it—and now I've completely forgotten the speech. You'll have to be satisfied with the present."

He opened the pouch, and I saw a profusion of colors.

"Oh, Marcus—they're lovely. But they must have cost nearly all your wages. The dyed goods are so expensive—"

43

"Who cares for that, as long as they please you? Here, take them."

One by one, I touched the silken veils he had drawn out. The first was scarlet, the second purple, the third pure ivory in hue. There were seven in all, he explained, for the seven hills of the city where we had met. I hugged them to my breast.

"I've never had a more beautiful gift, Marcus."

"They come from the East, where the yellow people live," he said. "The merchant assured me it was so. If I find out otherwise, I'll go back and bash his skull."

I looped the scarlet veil about my throat and let it fall over the breast of my stola.

"How does it look?"

Taking my hands in his, he said softly, "Pale and colorless, Salome, compared to your radiant face. Salome—"

"The Greens! Watch out, we've got company!"

The harsh cry rang from the track beyond the grove. Marcus sprang to his feet, scowling.

"Come to spy on us, no doubt. This could be unpleasant, Salome. I suggest you return to the city at once.

I knew very well that it could be unpleasant, since rivalry between the Blue and Green companies was especially strong, even violent at times, erupting into street brawls when plebians of each faction got to arguing. But I had no intention of missing the excitement.

Marcus raced ahead with swift strides to the place beside the track where the directors had gathered about the Blue chariot and team, which

44

had just been unhitched following the exercise run.

Down the road thundered four light racing chariots, each drawn by a yoked team of milk-white mares. From the breastplates and jeweled amulets the mares wore, and from the reckless manner in which the chariot drivers lashed their teams, it was apparent that the Blues were being visited by several hotheaded young noblemen of the Green persuasion.

One chariot pulled ahead of the others. A Blue handler crossing the road was almost run down. I hurried to the edge of the crowd where my father and Marcus stood, looking unhappy.

Someone whispered, "It's worse than we thought. It's Little Boots in person."

The leading chariot made a sharp turn and stopped, raising a cloud of dust. Several of the Blue directors started coughing. A spindly young man jumped down. His thin pale face and large liquid eyes gave him an unwholesome appearance. He swaggered through a lane that had opened in the crowd. He slapped a ringed hand on the flank of the Libyan.

"Don't tell me I've come too late to see the famed Centenarius run," he said. "You'll just have to give him another go around the track. I'm not accustomed to making jaunts into the country for nothing."

The young man said this last in such an overbearing way that it drew angry glances from the Blue directors. But they said nothing. The young man's three companions—burly louts, though they wore noble togas—had climbed down from their chariots and were regarding us with deri-

45

sive smiles. The young man was someone to be reckoned with in the politics of Rome, even though people said he was half mad.

An air of tension hung over the scene for a moment. I had a chance to study Little Boots, or Caligula, as the name is properly written. Son of the famed general Germanicus, and great nephew of the mighty Augustus Caesar, he had been a favorite with the legions in Gaul, where he had been raised while his father was serving there. The legionnaires had given him the nickname of Little Boots. I had never seen him up close before, and I perceived now that his feet were indeed tiny, clad in slippers sewn with pearls. Many said he would succeed the Emperor Tiberius when the latter died.

"Come, come," he said with a humorless grin. "Where are your tongues? Swallowed down into your guts at the sight of the opposition?"

"We welcome Gaius Caesar and his young friends to our stables," my father said stiffly. Little Boots listened with one eyebrow raised, contemptuous of being addressed by someone foreign-born. "However, the Libyan has run his course for the day. We cannot tire him further."

"Why not? He's bound to lose the big race anyway."

"May we beg leave to dispute the point?"

"You may beg it, but I'll be cursed if you'll get it," replied the young noble. His sycophants burst out laughing. The Blue directors wriggled uncomfortably.

Little Boots cast an eye over the crowd. "Where's your charioteer? I demand he take the beast at least one lap around the track. I want my friends to see how foolish it would be to bet on anything but the Green team. Granting they'd never bet that way in the first place. If they did, they might find themselves castrated and dumped in the Tiber."

Little Boots clapped a hand over his mouth and giggled.

Again his companions guffawed. The young nobleman began pushing people out of the way.

"Where's the charioteer? Bring him forth!"

Suddenly I noticed he was looking directly at Marcus. A strange smile was on his face. Once more the young noble repeated his order.

A muscle in Marcus' throat throbbed. His gaze grew bleak. I felt a sudden fear as Marcus stepped forward.

"Castor is ill and cannot drive today, your honor."

"I thought I recognized you," Little Boots said. He placed his fists on his hips. "Marcus Catullus, isn't it?"

"That's correct, your honor."

"Former slave and physician to Quintus Lucullus of the Greens?"

"You have an excellent memory," Marcus said in a polite voice.

"No, a very poor one. In fact, I wouldn't have bothered my head about you had it not been brought to my attention this very morning that you were now in the employ of the Blues. Since I'm a large stockholder in the Greens, I couldn't pass up an opportunity to verify that."

Meeting his gaze steadily, Marcus said nothing. There was a long pause.

"When your owner most graciously set you free,

you chose to desert the company to which you previously owned your loyalties, eh, Marcus?"

Marcus' brows knotted together. Rage was building up within him. I said a silent prayer that he would not forget his aging parents. A single command from the insufferable young man could deprive them of their freedom.

Still polite, Marcus said, "The Blues offered a wage I could not turn down, your honor."

"Even though accepting it might have displeased your former owner and his associates, who found your skills outstanding?"

"A man who is free must look out for himself."

"What about a dog turned loose? A dog that traitorously sinks its fangs into the hand that untied the leash?" Little Boots was enjoying the cruel baiting. "What should happen to him?"

"I don't know, your honor. I am a man, and could not speak for an animal. Perhaps you could."

One of the followers of Little Boots cursed. Little Boots raised one ringed hand to hold him back. He looked long and hard at Marcus.

Marcus did not flinch from the ugly stare. A false smile flitted across the slack lips of the young man.

"I shall remember your witticism, physician. I shall remember it for quite a long while, I assure you."

So saying, he flung about and leaped into his chariot. His followers hurried after him.

"Let's leave this place!" he called as he snatched up the traces. "It smells of dung."

With a cry to the team, he lashed out with the reins. The animals bolted. The long traces back-

48

lashed. The end of one of them laid open the cheek of a Blue handler standing too close. The poor man reeled, screaming, his face dripping blood. He would have fallen under the chariot wheels if Marcus had not jumped forward and pulled him back.

The chariots thundered off up the road to Rome. Marcus and the others clustered about the bleeding handler.

"Take this man to the stables immediately," Marcus ordered. "I'll look to his wounds."

A group of handlers rushed forward to bear the fallen man up the hill. Marcus joined them, having time to throw me only a single parting glance. In his eyes I still saw love shining, and I tried to answer that gaze, tried to show him how proud I was of his behavior in front of the arrogant Caligula.

Then he was gone up the hillside. My father came to my side, quickly saw me to the litter and hurried off to join the crowd.

On the long, jolting ride back into the city, with the late sun burning red near the horizon, I found myself touching the silken veils Marcus had given me. I held them one by one as if to draw strength from them. Terror had crept over me again, for I recalled a remark made by Little Boots—

He had been informed of the whereabouts of Marcus only this morning.

How was it that today, suddenly, Little Boots had learned of the position of an insignificant former slave of the Greens, who could be of little interest to him personally? Could someone have spitefully brought Marcus' work for the Blues to his attention?

It seemed incredible and yet I could think of no other explanation—nor any other culprit except—Thoth the Alexandrine.

Why had he done it? Had he acted at my mother's bidding? I knew she did not care for my relationship with Marcus, that she had other plans for me, and I was sure Thoth would have cooperated with her gladly, because there was no love lost between us.

Perhaps I was only imagining a plot where none existed. Yet somehow I couldn't bring myself to believe it. And I wondered whether the new development had any connection with the forthcoming arrival of Herod Antipas.

My mother, Thoth, Marcus—their lives were mysteriously tangled like the veils I held in my hands. Mine was tangled with theirs also—and became more tangled with each day that passed.

Chapter V

Banquet for Herod

To the music of lyres and timbrels, I danced for Herod Antipas on his second night in the Imperial City.

The occasion was a formal banquet in the peristyle of our house. Torches were held by slaves my mother had hired especially for the evening.

The crucial race was only a few days away, and I had scarcely seen my father since my visit to the grounds of the Blues. He and Marcus—of whose welfare I learned by means of messages carried back and forth by Gemma—had been occupying themselves night and day at the stables.

As a result, the task of the banquet had fallen to my mother. She had spared no expense, as my father angrily pointed out during a loud quarrel I overheard a few hours before the feasting began.

Shrilly my mother ordered my father to be silent—wasn't our guest exhausted from arriving with his retinue in the middle of the preceding night? Not wanting to listen to more, I hurried past the entrance to my father's office. Spying me, my mother left him with one last retort.

"It seems I've married a purse instead of a man. And an empty one at that."

I had a glimpse of my father seated upon the heavy chest in which he kept his valuables, his face twisted into an expression of impotent rage. Then my mother hurried me along to inspect the expensive and immodestly sheer linen stola dyed Tyrian purple which she had purchased for me.

"Dance well for our guest, Salome." Herodias held up the new garment to judge its fit. "Ah, you should see him! A lion of a man!" Her eyes sparkled with unnatural excitement.

"You shouldn't talk of him that way, Mother. Didn't father say Antipas was married?"

"Married to a barbarian. A savage! Her name is Nefer. Her father is some petty king of a desert tribe called the Nabateans. Obviously she can't be much if the name of her sire Aretas has never before been heard along the Tiber. But praise to the gods, Antipas didn't bring her with him. Now remember, dear, when you meet him, speak in a manner befitting a young lady and say nothing that would place us in disfavor."

With that she vanished, off to berate the cooks preparing the meal. I was more confused and disheartened than ever. What possible gain could our family reap from ingratiating ourselves with Antipas? None that I could see.

But I would still present myself well, for I took pride in my appearance. I had Gemma arrange my hair three times until it was perfect. While the lyres hummed gently in the evening air, I crept to the edge of the peristyle and looked out between two of the torch bearers. Waiting to be summoned, I had ample opportunity to study our guest.

At first I could not believe that my mother had called him a lion. Although stocky of body, he seemed pale and dissipated. He reclined in the left-hand place of honor on the curved dining couch for which my mother had paid a great deal. In the center lay my father, Herodias on his right. Before them the round dining table was set with bowls of oysters and uncooked vegetables, together with the remains of several waterfowl and a whole suckling. The diners had finished the first two courses, and launched into the dessert. Pastries and nuts were passed together with flagons of mulsum.

Herod Antipas seemed to have drunk a great deal. His chin shone sticky with the mixture of honey and wine. Gobbets of food littered his section of the couch, as well as the front of his russet cloak with its ostentatious brooch of sapphires. He was stouter than my father, and bore little family resemblance; I judged him to be in his early forties. He talked loudly, had black eyes, and was constantly fondling and twisting his thick black beard in a most ungenteel way.

"Bring forth this pride of your household,
53

Herodias," he said after a loud belch. "I'm sick of looking at sailors and litter carriers." He drank more mulsum, spilling some into his beard. "Although your presence by my side at this handsome banquet has done much to relieve my complaint."

"Our only desire is to bring pleasure to our relative," my mother replied with a smile. Her pearl-sewn stola had slipped at one shoulder, revealing too much of her large, firm breast, which Antipas did not miss. She seemed unconcerned. Enviously she studied his splendid garments. Sunk in moody silence, my father picked at the leftovers in a bowl of fruit.

"Salome! Come greet our guest from beyond the sea."

Head downward, I went forward in response to my mother's call. I said the polite and proper things, but I didn't care for the way Antipas let his gaze linger on my body. I wished Herodias had not insisted upon my gown being so thin. Antipas took my hand in his.

"You're a very fair child. A welcome and rewarding sight."

"Thank you, sir."

I turned away with too much eagerness, and signaled the slave musicians. They began to beat the timbrels with their naked palms and pluck the lyres to mix melody with the rhythm.

In dancing I had always found a strange release, a feeling of being someone other than myself. I had been trained in all the traditional modes as part of my schooling, and was able to mime various stories. For Antipas I had chosen to play a shepherdess visited by the wing-footed

54

messenger of the gods on his journeys round the skies above the Roman countryside. But I performed it badly, missing steps, falling out of time with the timbrels, even stumbling once and nearly losing my balance.

Antipas didn't seem to notice. He hardly lifted his gaze to my face, staring at my breasts over the rim of his cup.

I grew more and more nervous. I strained to catch the end of the melody, and when it came, averted my eyes and quickly retired to my couch feeling I had shamed myself.

Antipas hitched himself on his elbow and turned to my mother. "I envy the man who takes that child to wife."

"I've tried to train her well in the feminine arts women must know," my mother replied, with such a display of false modesty that I wanted to hide my face.

"I wish we had a few like your daughter in Galilee to tame the ruffians roaming the roads and terrorizing the citizens with their religious nonsense. A sweet face might be the answer. Certainly the lash and the sword have done little good." Antipas scowled. "That's because I have hardly any authority. The situation, of course, is far worse in Judea and Samaria."

At last my father stirred himself. "Who rules there?"

"The procurator Pontius Pilate." Antipas glowered. It took few brains to know that he had just pronounced the name of his worst enemy.

"Not a tetrarch, I take it?"

"No. More on the order of a military governor." Antipas knocked over his goblet in disgust. "But who am I to demean him? I, whom my noble father—and yours, Philip, don't forget—considered unfit to rule all the land of Jordan? Carving it up in pieces was a hideous mistake, though. The Emperor will see that when I report to him."

"How soon will you be journeying to Capri to see him?" asked my mother.

"Much as I'd like to meet with Tiberius at once, I have financial transactions to attend to here in Rome. I doubt if I'll get away before the Saturnalia."

"Then you must accept the hospitality of this house during your entire stay."

In the gleam of the torches the face of Antipas looked almost lustful. "That would please me well. But won't you become tired of my company during the interval? The festival of Saturn is still many weeks away."

"I could never tire of hearing about your efforts to reunite the kingdom of the Herods," my mother replied softly.

"Just what exactly has prompted your long journey?" my father asked. "So far you haven't told us specifically."

Antipas cast him a shrewd glance, aware that my father was baiting him ever so slightly. "I'm to report to Tiberius on the disordered situation in the Imperial provinces. To put it bluntly, I was requested to inform him personally of the efficiency of the procurator of Judea."

My father smiled. "In other words, you're spying?"

"Brother, there's always been precious little ambition in your blood, so I won't rebuke you for

56

putting it in those words. But I consider my task a sacred one. I not only intend to serve the Emperor, I intend to make him recognize that chaos will prevail beyond the sea until a single, strong hand is put in charge! From the Sea of Galilee to the Sea of Judgment we've got armed bands of Jewish zealots stirring up trouble. They can only be put down by force—which is best administered by a single man, a king who can rule from Iturea to Judea and—"

"Sir," I interrupted, "I don't understand all those names and places. Would it be unseemly for me to ask you to describe the territories of which you speak?"

"I'll be happy to describe them, Salome. Draw near."

Chapter VI

Ambition

He swept aside several bowls and saltcellars.
Then he overturned another goblet of red wine.
Some of it splattered on my father's best white
linen toga. My father's face darkened. He was
reaching the end of his patience with his half-
brother, an alien creature who smelled oddly of
spices and heavy male sweat.

Antipas, however, didn't bother to apologize.
With his finger he traced a vertical streak in the
spilled wine.

The line, he explained, represented the river
called Jordan, running approximately south to

north. He also drew in the Sea of Galilee, and southward the brackish Sea of Judgment. Westward of the latter lay Jerusalem, center of the territories ruled by the Roman procurator Pilate.

On the eastern side of the Jordan, and northward, were the lands for which Antipas was responsible. He finally sketched in the northern provinces of Trachonitis and Iturea, governed by Philip the Tetrarch.

"Even you, Herod Phillip," he said, "have ambition compared to our milksop half-brother in Trachonitis. He speaks softly as a woman, and his hands have never known a sword. I don't worry much about him, frankly. He's so old and feeble, he can't live long. It's Pilate who's the thorn. Pilate is far from old, and he's intent upon remaining in his post."

"Surely you have the better command of the whole situation," my mother said to him. "And besides, it's only right that the kingdom of Herod the Great be restored to one of his children."

Antipas nodded. "I often think of our father. I wonder what whim caused him to draw up the will denying the succession to any of his sons." Antipas stared gloomily into his mulsum. "I also think, too, if I'd been present at the moment he drew the will, I would have killed him."

My father looked disbelieving. "You must be joking."

"By the gods, no! To throw away such riches as his kingdom once possessed—to slice it up in pieces for any weakling like Philip the Tetrarch to ruin—"

"Our guest is right," my mother said. "To make great gains, great deeds are necessary."

Antipas swung around. It was as though he saw her for the first time. A flush crept up my mother's cheeks. Her breasts jutted immodestly beneath her gown, rising and falling more rapidly than before.

"Exactly, Herodias," Antipas said to her. "You understand."

"For my part, I'd sooner leave the punishment of local thieves to the legions," my father commented.

"Thieves?" Antipas leaped up and strode across the peristyle, his cloak swirling out as he made a flamboyant gesture. "The Sicarii are far more than thieves! Do you know what the name means? The dagger-carriers. Time and again soldiers who wander too far from their encampment are found with their throats slit and their tongues carved out. The Jewish rebels have but one purpose—to overthrow the law of Rome and establish the rule of their angry god, a diety they call Yahweh. To make matters worse, other Jewish sects send traveling preachers into all the provinces. They criticize Rome and harangue the Jews about returning to the old ways before it's too late. Three rulers can't deal with such a chaotic situation, especially when one is a weakling like Philip of Trachonitis and the other a schemer like Pilate."

Wearily, my father shook his head. "Life is so short, Antipas. Why fret over who rules a piece of arid foreign soil? There's little enough time for men to enjoy themselves."

"He means that horsemanship is more interesting than kingship," said Herodias.

"You may be as caustic as you wish, my dear. But, yes, I do believe that."

"Then all I can say is, you've lived too long in the soft ways of Rome, Phillip," Antipas put in.

"I think you're both mad with this endless talk of power and more power," my father replied, his voice sharper.

"That's why you'll never be more than a minor stockholder in a shoddy company whose only accomplishment is the appeasement of public taste!" Herodias blazed.

My father stared at her. Again I found myself wishing he would strike her as she sat facing him in open defiance, her cheeks red with some strange lust Antipas had generated. But no—my father was always drawn inward into himself, and bore his wounds silently. Gathering the hem of his toga in his hand, he addressed himself to our guest in a quiet voice.

"If you'll excuse me, the wine has made me a little tired. I beg leave to go."

Grumbling like a bear, Antipas gestured him away and lurched back to the dining table. My mother grasped his hands and pulled him down to her side. She asked him to tell her more of the strife-torn land whose crown he sought. My father's somehow pathetic figure disappeared into the shadows.

On an impulse I leaped up to run after him. Herodias paid no attention. I had barely reached the colonnade when a figure stepped into my path. I leaped back, stifling a cry.

"Remain, Mistress. You have pleased Antipas."

In the smoky light of the blowing torches, the

eyes of Thoth the Alexandrine gleamed as brightly as those of the cat on his shoulder.

"I want to speak with my father. Stand aside—"

"No, Mistress. Return to the table."

"How dare you—!"

"Return, Salome—without further protest. Your mother wishes you to please her guest."

"So now it's *her* guest is it?"

He said nothing.

"If you don't get out of my way this instant, I'll have you whipped."

"I think not."

His lips curved in a smile.

I raised my arm to strike him. Swift as an adder, his hand caught my wrist and gripped so fiercely I thought the bone would snap. On his shoulder the cat arched its back, bared its teeth, and hissed.

Thoth twisted my hand until I was ready to cry out. "I think not, Mistress," he repeated. "There'll be no lash on my back because I'm not an ordinary slave. You'd best remember that."

His words were so pointed I completely lost my temper.

"Is that a threat?"

"A threat?" he echoed as if surprised. "Why, no. I would never presume to threaten my mistress."

"But you'd threaten Marcus Catullus, wouldn't you?"

Thoth's eyes, deep in folds of fat, blinked once. "You mean the young physician you fancy? I'm not acquainted with him, Mistress, other than to recognize his name. I'm sure I don't know what you mean by your remark."

"You beastly—"

But my tongue went wooden in my mouth as the sight of his oiled, sexless body filled me with revulsion. Thoughts of Marcus flashed through my mind—thoughts of his parents, of their tenuous freedom, and his. Thoth let me go. I spun and ran across the colonnade, out into the peristyle. Antipas was again stalking up and down, goblet in his hand, exclaiming at the top of his lungs:

"There *will* be a king beyond the Mare Nostrum, I promise you that. Should his throne have to be built on the rotting bodies of a thousand rivals—there will be a king."

He paused, gazing at my mother who sat enraptured at his feet.

"There will be a queen, too. A queen worthy of the name."

"Your wife, Nefer?" Herodias asked.

"I said a queen, my lady, not a wife. There is a difference."

I glanced back over my shoulder. Thoth had vanished. I approached the dining table and Antipas bade me drink with them. To dull my fears, I did so. I listened to him rave of how he would be King of the Jews long into the night.

Chapter VII

Thunder in the Circus Maximus

At the fourth hour of the day of the race on which my father had wagered nearly all that was left of his personal fortune, I set out in a litter for the great Circus Maximus.

My father and Marcus had been at the Circus all night readying the Blue entry. Herodias and Antipas had risen at dawn and gone there with a party of slaves, so as to be present for the very first races early in the morning. These, and all the subsequent races including the eighth—the one in which Castor would drive the Centenarius—they would watch from the family box. I went alone because I had no desire to see them whispering together as they did almost every day now.

The streets leading to the Circus were deserted except for soldiers of the legions stationed on every corner to prevent riotous behavior and looting. The sponsor of the games, a senator by the name of Publius Scriptus Capito, had spared no expense, and for blocks around the Circus the ramshackle apartments of the poorer classes were bedecked with flowers. Petals formed a carpet beneath the feet of the slaves bearing my litter. Even from a great distance, the roar of the crowd—possibly as many as four hundred thousand people—echoed down the streets like thunder.

Soon this bellow was punctuated by the cries of souvenir vendors. They swarmed around the litter, offering scarves of green or red or blue or white. As we drew still closer to the Circus, I saw legionnaires hustling off groups of bloodied rioters from the Red and White factions. On race day, the whole of Rome worshipped at the shrine of recklessness.

The litter bearers carried me around to the staging area beneath the stands. In the clamor of horses and man, among shadowy dung-tainted pens, I sought the Blue section and dismissed the litter. I shoved along through broken chariots and limping charioteers, unlucky losers in earlier contests, until I spied the pearl-decorated manes of the Libyan and the other three horses Castor would drive.

Attendants were already tying up the tails of the beasts and putting on the blue ribbons and the heavy golden breastplates. Other slaves busily polished the gleaming wood of the chariot.

My father looked haggard. He greeted me curtly.

"Don't look so glum, Father. I know the Blues will have a win today."

"Not without a charioteer," he snapped.

"What?"

"Castor has disappeared, Salome." I turned and saw the new speaker—Marcus. His face, too, was bleak. "You'd best go to the family box. Things are in a turmoil down here. No one's seen Castor since sunset yesterday."

"Have you searched the camps of the other factions again?" my father asked.

"Thoroughly. Little Boots is already crowing over a Green victory."

My father scowled. "Is it possible that young fool Castor could have gone to one of the wine shops and drunk himself senseless? He's been acting strangely these past few days—completely ignoring your prescriptions, Marcus. He might be sitting a block from here right this moment. He's always had too strong a love for the grape."

"I'll gather men and search," said Marcus.

"Be swift. We've precious little time before the race."

A swelling roar erupted over our heads. One of the handlers raced up. "The seventh race is over. Luxus of the Greens took it. The procurators are already watering and raking the sand."

"Isn't it possible," I suggested, "that Castor has gone to the little temple of Venus of the Sea, out on the Spine, to say a prayer? All the charioteers go there at one time or another before a race, don't they?"

"We've been there long ago," Marcus said. "You won't find this a pleasant place unless we locate Castor soon."

He gave me a peck on the cheek and tried to smile, but his eyes were unhappy. He rushed off to recruit a group of men. A few moments later the men disappeared toward the nearby avenues, crashing open the doors of wine shops without ceremony.

I wanted to say a word of reassurance to my father, even though I felt little cause for hope, but he had turned away and was wandering by himself, kicking the packed earth and shaking his head. I set off through the stands to find my mother.

Stepping into the sunlight on the upper level, I marveled anew at the magnificence of the great Circus. As always, its beauty and immensity were overwhelming. Down the center of the gigantic oval ran the Spine, around which each race was run. Statues of the gods and goddesses rose from it, reflecting the sun. Jets of perfumed water sprayed from fountains at either end. Near the center, the ball atop the great Egyptian obelisk burned like a hot yellow eye.

At both ends of the Spine, just inside the metae—masonry cones which served as bumpers for the chariots swinging around the turns—erectors were clambering up marble columns. Atop each was a crossbar. One held eggs made of marble, in honor of Castor and Pollux, and another carried marble dolphins, symbolizing Neptune, the patron of horses. The erectors put seven eggs and seven dolphins into place at the start of

67

each race, and took down one for each of the seven laps.

The crowd was more excited than I had ever seen it before. Hippomania was the popular name for this wild enthusiasm, and today it manifested itself more violently than ever. I passed two freedmen hysterically offering themselves to slave dealers in order to raise funds. In another box a woman was writhing on her back in the last extremes of sexual arousal.

But the most appalling sight awaited me in the family box.

Under a canopy held by our slaves, my mother sat beside Antipas as trumpeters marched out upon the track and blew blasts to signal the eighth race. Even though I sensed the presence of Thoth at the entrance to the box, I couldn't take my eyes from my mother's face.

Her skin gleamed with perspiration. Her gown was awry and her cheeks flushed in the manner of the writhing woman I had seen a few moments before. She was touching Antipas' cheek and fondling him in the most intimate way. His ringed hands in turn crawled over her breasts as she caressed his ear with her tongue.

"You will be more comfortable beneath the canopy," came Thoth's voice in my ear. His bald head ran with sweat, and his tunic was stained at the arm pits. He looked like some night-creature suddenly dragged to the light to die.

He gestured into the box. "Join your mother, Mistress. The race is about to begin."

Again I glanced at Herodias, horrified at the way she continued to caress Antipas in plain sight of those seated all around. Of course the crowd didn't really care—such sexual play was considered a routine part of the madness of race day. Yet I thought I saw not just outright lust in her behavior, but dreadful ambition as well.

I exclaimed to Thoth, "It's your influence that makes her behave in this disgusting way."

"Be silent," he whispered. "Go into the box and say no more. If you are a sensible girl, you'll make no trouble for her."

"Make no trouble . . . ?" I gasped. "Haven't I a voice in my own family?"

His tiny eyes glittered with amusement. "No, Mistress, not any longer."

My mother laughed loudly at some lewd remark Antipas had made. Thoth took a step forward. The stink of his body—sweat mingled with perfume—rose up to gag me. I whirled and fled the crowd.

Down and down I ran, wanting only to escape, to blot out the memory of what I had seen. At last I stumbled and fell against a pillar in the shadows beneath the stands. Overhead another hurrah went up from the mob. The trumpets pealed again. I passed a hand over my eyes, dizzy and frightened, and wondered what I should do now that I had seen my mother's infidelity flagrantly displayed.

Suddenly my attention was caught by two figures huddling behind the next pillar. One I recognized as a member of the group that had accompanied Little Boots to the track of the Blues. Despite the heat, the other wore a cloak partially concealing his face. But I recognized him.

It was Castor.

What was he doing with a functionary of the

Greens. As I watched, he nodded while the Green noble smiled and whispered.

I darted away through the shadows hurrying to the place where I had left my father.

The hour had grown later than I imagined. The four teams for the next race had already been led out into the Circus, where handlers were parading them under the editor's box. The chariots had also been rolled out. I ran down a dark tunnel smelling of horse urine. At the end I glimpsed my father, Marcus, and several of the Blue directors.

"Marcus!" He ran to meet me. Panting, I fell against him. "You didn't find your charioteer—"

"No. We searched every dram shop in the neighborhood. Not a sign of him."

"I think I can tell you with whom he's—"

"Look, here he comes!" someone shouted.

Before I could say another word, the Blue director who had made the outcry rushed past me back along the tunnel. He was followed by my father and the others. They swarmed about Castor, slapping him on the back and asking questions. Castor blinked and swayed, his face an unhealthy gray, his forehead glistening with sweat.

"In the name of almighty Jove, where have you been?" my father demanded.

"Sick," he replied. "Sick puking in the Tiber, if you must know. Stand aside. Let me lean against the wall. I've got to rest a moment."

"If your drinking has cost us this race—" my father began.

"Drinking, nothing!" Castor snapped. "I've touched no wine in a week. Marcus ordered me not to. When I ate dinner at the Inn of Parthia last evening, they must have served tainted meat.

70

I retched all night, and had the fever, and finally fainted dead away just before dawn. If I hadn't fallen off my couch an hour ago and gotten quite a jolt, I'd probably still be sleeping. Gods, I feel awful," he concluded, massaging his belly as he threw off his cloak.

He already wore his tunic, leather cap and greaves. Shoving my father aside, he lurched toward one of the massive doors which opened on either side of the tunnel.

"Let me lie on a couch a moment and I'll be all right."

"There's no time—" said one of the Blue directors.

"Heed his wishes!" Marcus said, "otherwise we'll have no entry at all." Castor reeled through the door and slammed it behind him. I could not keep silent.

"Father, Marcus—listen. I think Castor is planning to betray you. I think he's lying about his sickness. Just moments ago I saw him talking under the stands with one of the Green nobles who came to the track with Caligula."

My father seized my arm. "Daughter, don't make jokes at a time like this."

"I swear by Jove Thunderer! I saw him!"

"Castor has never shown the slightest sign of disloyalty," Marcus objected.

"That's not to say there isn't a first time," my father replied. "You know how well-financed the Greens are. What fat bribes they could offer—"

Another burst of trumpets sounded from the rack.

"There's the call for drivers," someone exclaimed.

71

"Do we dare trust Castor?" my father asked. "I say no."

"His actions certainly sound suspicious," responded another director. "But still—"

"Do you accuse my daughter of lying?"

"No, no, of course not. I vote against Castor, too."

"But who will drive . . . ?" began another director.

Quickly my father stepped to the door through which Castor had vanished. He slammed home the iron bolt so that the charioteer was locked in. Looking grim he said:

"Fetch Olipor. He wanted his chance—he'll have it."

"Olipor! Olipor!"

The cry echoed along the dismal tunnel as Castor set up a fierce protest inside the chamber. He cursed and shouted, and rattled the door, but the iron bolt held fast. Handlers rushed back and forth, bringing necessary equipment and keeping watch on the track. Finally young Olipor appeared, his face flushed.

Men helped him into his tunic and cap and thrust a dagger into his hands so that he might cut the traces if necessary. Then he was rushed out toward the chariot as the Blue directors shouted encouragement.

Marcus found a moment to come to my side. Strain showed in the dark shadows beneath his eyes. He took my arm. As we hurried to the tunnel's mouth, he said:

"Olipor has never driven in an important race before. He's quick and talented, but he's going against experienced professionals. Are you certain of what you saw, Salome?"

"There was no mistake. The Green agent seemed to be trying to bargain with him."

"Then we have no choice. If Castor deliberately planned to lose the race—" Glumly Marcus shook his head. "After all the weeks and months we've worked, after all the money the company has wagered on a win—to have this happen!"

"Olipor will drive splendidly, Marcus. I'm sure of it."

"I wish *I* were."

We moved out of the tunnel to a point on the sand a safe distance from the starting stalls. From here we could observe the crucial start. Many races were actually won or lost in those first moments when the teams vied for position along the Spine.

I had never watched a race from this vantage point before. And the spectacle made me gasp. The great stands swept upward, packed with screaming Romans. Purple banners flew in the breeze above the editor's box. Sunlight gleamed on the chariots and the trappings of the teams.

Since the trumpets had already sounded the call for drivers, the other charioteers had already mounted. Olipor scrambled up into his light vehicle, took his whip in his right hand and assumed the wide-legged driving stance. The handlers wrapped the traces around his waist, then leaped clear.

The starters swarmed onto the track, swung the heads of the left-hand horses around and led them to the stalls. The Libyan occupied his customary position, unyoked as usual.

A hump-backed dwarf employed by the Blues because he was rumored to have magical communication with dumb animals scurried about crying shrill entreaties at the horses. The Libyan pawed and snorted as the starters tried to force him into the stall. Then the Red team balked. Several flicks of the charioteer's whip got them in position. At last the four chariots were all in their proper stalls.

Instantly the gates were slammed shut. The handlers jumped back. When the gates opened, they would open all at once, worked by a complicated system of ropes and weighted bags. Inside the stalls could be heard the thudding of hoofs and the neighing of the penned horses as one by one the charioteers called off their readiness. A vast hue fell, sweeping from the near to the far end of the amphitheatre. In the editor's box a stout figure in purple rose and raised one arm.

I gripped Marcus' hand. Directly ahead, to the right of the Spine, judges stretched the Alba Linea tight across the track, at a height designed to throw a running horse. The perfumed fountains splashed in the silence. Marcus returned the pressure of my hand. The editor's hand came down.

Chapter VIII

Fortunes of the Greens

With a crash, the gates sprang open. The four teams bolted out. A roar rocked the stadium. In a cloud of dust the chariots hurtled down the track, straight for the white rope.

The Red team slowed perceptibly. The driver had made a quick judgment that the start would be declared improper, because the Green driver had already tried unsuccessfully to foul Olipor by locking wheels. The Red driver's judgment was poor. He lost his place in front while Olipor drove recklessly, cutting to the left for the inner lane.

Still the Alba Linea did not drop. I covered my face.

"Marcus, he'll be killed!"

"No, by the Thunderer!" Marcus shouted. "It's a fair start!"

His voice was drowned out by a chorus of cheers from my father at the other Blues:

"A fair start!"

"Olipor's along the Spine!"

"Look at him drive! He's halfway to the metae already!"

I saw that Olipor had indeed gained the inner lane just as the white rope dropped, and was even now flicking the Libyan's back to turn him rightly around the Spine at the far end. Side by side and a length behind him were the White and Green teams. The Red driver was just pulling away from the fallen starting rope.

By the time Olipor completed his first lap he had stretched his lead to three lengths.

As he went thundering back up the Spine, the erectors scrambled down the pillars with the first of the eggs and dolphins. The Blues were already slapping one another on the back and congratulating themselves.

For two more laps the Blue chariot remained in the lead. The spirited Libyan showed his sure-footedness on the sharp turns, pulling to the left at precisely the right moment. The chariot came within a hairsbreadth of the metae, its off-wheel rising high in the air, then crashing down as the power of the Libyan's stride dragged the rest of the team around the turn and down the Spine.

Suddenly, the crowd gave an explosive shout. The Green charioteer swung in to ram the White as both teams neared the end of the Spine closest to the stalls.

The White driver tried to fend off his adversary but the Green driver was too skillful. He hooked his wheel into his opponent's, lashed his team, and swung them out.

The White wheel snapped and spun off the axle. The Green team leaped forward out of danger. The White chariot broke its yoke and crashed full speed into the Spine.

The White driver was thrown into the air and bashed against the Spine headfirst. His skull burst open. He fell onto the track like a twisted doll. The citizens in the stands shrieked at the sight of blood.

The maddened horses of the White team reared and pawed over the charioteer, crushing his bones and lacerating his chest. I dug my fingers into Marcus' arm.

The Blue directors gave no thought to the dead man. Their concern was with Olipor. He was racing down the far side of the Spine, unaware of the wreckage littering the track just around the turn. The Green team was coming up fast, trying to close the gap.

A handler had rushed forward to cut the White team free of its traces. He succeeded just as Olipor rounded the metae. My stomach wrenched. The code of the games required the handler to look out for himself.

My father turned pale when Olipor spied the handler and pulled hard on the traces. Olipor swung the team to the right to avoid the man, almost bringing the chariot to a halt.

"The fool, the wretched fool!" my father cried,

tears running down his cheeks. "Is he trying to ruin us? Drive, Olipor, you piece of dung! Start your team! *Run over that man!*"

Olipor managed to avoid the handler and get his chariot started again. But the delay had been costly. The Green chariot had gained the inner lane.

The elation of the Blues turned to dismay as the Green team thundered only a single length behind Olipor. Olipor drove steadily again in the outer lane.

"Why doesn't he swing over and block the green driver?" Marcus raged. "Has he forgotten everything he knows?"

"Marcus—quickly!" said a voice at our elbow. It was a groom, wide-eyed and frightened. "Castor is screaming like a wild man. I fear he'll do himself harm if we don't unlock the door."

"Very well, release him," Marcus said. "He can't hurt our cause now."

The Green and Blue chariots vanished in the dust at the Spine's far end. My father wailed to the gods that Olipor had forgotten an elementary strategy of racing and let the Green team draw abreast without blocking it. Just then a flushed, disheveled Castor raced from the tunnel. He seized Marcus and whirled him around.

"Why was I locked in that room? If you were trying to throw the race away, you did a neat job. May the gods strike you down for your stupidity—"

Castor stalked up to the group of Blue directors.

"Don't you see? This is exactly what the Greens wanted—Olipor in our chariot! Is he winning? I can see from your faces that he isn't. I could have pulled it off—but you put a *traitor* up!"

"Traitor!" my father exclaimed. "Fine talk for one who sold out to the Greens himself."

Castor made a threatening gesture. "Who accuses me of selling out? You, Herod Philip? I ought to smash your teeth back into your head."

"Liar! *Cheat!*" my father cried. "My own daughter saw you conspiring with a member of Caligula's faction just before the race. Do you deny it?"

"Deny I talked to Primus Scipio? Of course I don't. Can't you simpletons see beyond the ends of your noses? He tried to bribe me to feign illness—so Olipor could drive!"

Up the Spine, the Green and Blue teams raced toward us, jeweled manes flying. The erectors hung from the crossbars, eagerly waiting to pull down the sixth egg and dolphin. Not a single person in the Circus Maximus was seated. All stood howling with one mad voice.

Castor swung toward me. "I wish your dear daughter could also have heard me turn down the Green's offer. I could have played sick easily enough—in fact my gut still aches from that bad meat." He shielded his eyes against the sun. "Look! Here comes your traitor—trying to swing the Libyan too soon. If this isn't the place he wrecks you all, I don't know racing."

The Green team swung tightly around the metae. Olipor took the turn in the outer lane as though he were taking it on the inner.

Castor pointed triumphantly. "He's even got his knife ready to cut the traces!"

My eyes were not that sharp. I saw only the veering of the Blue chariot back toward the Spine. Its wheel grazed the basreliefs on the conical stone bumper, then crumpled as the Libyan horse was crowded against the Spine by the force of the turning team.

Olipor fought with the traces. The chariot struck the Spine full force. When Olipor tried to leap free, the traces tangled about his shoulders. Above the frightened screams of the horses rose his piercing scream. He fell beneath the hooves, flailing and fighting for his life.

The right-hand horse snapped free and galloped off, dragging a length of the traces behind him. This length had gotten looped about Olipor's neck. The charioteer's body bumped along through the dust, a bloodied wreck.

Now the Green faction was cheering thunderously. The Blue supporters had fallen silent. My father took a shaky step forward, his shoulders trembling.

"The Libyan—the Centenarius—the yoke has gored him—"

With my knuckles between my teeth, bitten nearly to the bone, I saw that what he said was true. In the crash, the end of the yoke had stabbed into the side of the great horse. The Libyan lay on his side screaming with pain and thrashing his hoofs. My father turned away and was sick upon the sand.

"Gods!" he whispered after a moment. "Someone—Marcus—go kill the animal."

Ashen, Marcus grabbed a short sword from one of the handlers and dashed out onto the track. The Green team made its turn around the

Spine and passed the Blue wreckage. The Green driver never gave so much as a look at the body of the traitor who had lost his life through his own inept driving.

Marcus delivered the death stroke to the valiant Libyan. Amid tumultuous applause, the Green driver wheeled his chariot up to the editor's box to accept the victory garland.

"Wiped out," one of the Blue directors murmured. "Just like that."

The Libyan gave one last dying scream. My father covered his ears. I felt the warm taste of blood in my mouth, blood from my own lips. My head swam. My father raised his head and stared at me.

In his eyes I saw unconcealed hatred.

Sobbing, I ran into the dark tunnel beneath the Circus while the Green faction thundered its victory chant.

BOOK TWO

GALILEE

Chapter I

Adultery at Saturnalia

"Mistress how long can you lie alone, brooding in the dark? Let me light the brazier."

Gemma had stolen silently into my chamber while I drowsed. She struck sparks and blew on them to light the charred hickory wood.

Gradually warmth began to radiate from the little stove. Gemma transferred fire to a rush light which dispelled some of the shadows in the corners.

The light showed how thin Gemma had become. Food for the slaves had grown shorter and shorter since the disastrous race. Creditors ap-

peared every day in my father's office. One by one
the slaves were led away and offered in the mart,
until only three remained in the house. I did not
count Thoth, for I no longer considered him a
slave, but rather some sinister extension of my
mother's personality. Lately he had taken to
stalking about with a lordliness that would have
earned any other bound man a thrashing for in-
solence.

"Let's put on our shawls and go for a walk in
the streets," Gemma suggested. "The merrymak-
ers are everywhere. You ought to see the cos-
tumes and the masks, Mistress."

"I have no desire to see any part of the festival, Gemma."

"Forgive me for saying it, but you just can't
continue to sleep morning and night as you've
done for weeks. It's already the middle of the
twelfth month, and the winds are growing sharp.
You need activity to warm the blood."

"Nothing can warm my blood while I live in
this house."

Gemma knelt at my feet. She shyly clasped my
right hand.

"But at least they haven't sold me, Mistress.
We've had so many good times together. We'll
have them again, if you'll only free yourself of
gloom."

"Gloom suits this place," I said. "Be quiet a
moment and just listen."

In a moment she understood. Not a sound could
be heard except for the distant clatter of a shut-
ter banging on the upper story, not a voice save
those of the revelers streaming through the

streets in celebration of the festival of the holy seed-sower.

"Remember what a happy house this was only a year ago, Gemma?"

She nodded, a tear gleaming on her cheek. I lost myself in memory of it. "Laughter wherever you turned. Not even the coming of winter could spoil the joy of Saturnalia, with masters waiting upon servants and wine flowing and every room bright with lamps—"

"Now there aren't even many lamps," Gemma sighed. "The auctioneers took the last of the large bronze ones away this morning—along with the water clock and the table of pink marble."

"Then it's worse than I thought. Father loved the form and color of that table more than any of his possessions—except the dead Libyan. It's my fault he lost them both."

"Mistress, stop blaming yourself for what happened at the Circus. Anyone would have come to the same conclusion about what you saw. You can't bear the guilt forever."

"Why not? My father believes the guilt is rightly mine."

"Has he told you so?"

"He's told me nothing. He hasn't spoke a word to me since that day."

"Not one?"

"The few times I've passed him in the halls, he's looked away. Before Drusus was sold, he told me Father spends most of his time in the taverns. He hasn't been in the house for the past two nights. *And it's my fault.*"

"Mistress, you must stop saying that. It's true he suffered a great shock. But he's a sensible

87

man. When he recovers and looks at things reasonably, he won't continue to hold you responsible."

"I don't believe that, Gemma."

"But it's true! Your father's going through a period of melancholy because he's incurred so many debts, and he's been forced to strip the house nearly bare to pay them. You should try to console him."

"Oh? When he won't even speak to me?"

"Can't your mother help, then?"

"My mother is completely occupied with entertaining our house guest," I said in a bitter tone.

"You just say that because you've never gotten along with Herodias."

"Gemma, how dare you!"

"I'm sorry, Mistress. But I have to speak out. This household is in terrible straits. You can have me beaten for saying it, but it won't change the fact that if you want to help your father, you shouldn't shrink from approaching your mother. After all, she is his wife. And she's no monster carved out of stone—she's a woman of flesh and feelings—just as you are."

Ambitious flesh, I thought somberly. Wanton feelings.

But I held my tongue and didn't chastise Gemma any further. After I'd thought it over, I realized there was some merit in the slave girl's suggestion. The least my mother could do was rebuff me, leaving the situation unchanged. On the other hand, if by chance I caught her in one of her rare good moods, she might have a suggestion about breaking down the barrier of ill feeling my father had raised between us.

With more encouragement from Gemma, I did up my hair with my last few ivory pins—there was no money to buy more—these days—and set out across the peristyle for my mother's chambers.

A slate-colored sky spread overhead. In the street, revelers sang and shouted. As I passed into the antechamber of my mother's quarters I heard a band of them hammer at the street gate, crying for free wine.

A heavy hanging separated the antechamber from the cubicle where my mother kept her sleeping couch. I stopped short. Through the folds I heard Herodias talking to someone.

Had my father returned? Elated, I raised a hand to thrust the hanging aside. Then my hand turned cold.

The man was Antipas.

"—your answer," his coarse voice rumbled. "My business in Rome is completed. I've gotten a dispatch from Sejanus on Capri. Tiberius is ready to receive me as soon as I can travel to the island."

I heard my mother reply with the voice of a woman aroused by passion.

"Can you have any doubts about my answer, Antipas?"

There followed a period in which all I could hear was the sound of rustling garments, and soft moans from my mother's lips. I stared at the hanging as if it were a lattice crawling with asps. I wanted to flee, yet I was somehow unable to move.

Inside, Antipas laughed.

"I thank the stars I came to Rome, Herodias.

Else I'd never have met you. You'll be a fit queen to sit beside me, once you're rid of that miserable husband of yours and I bar Nefer from my palace."

"You said her father Aretas was a fierce warrior. Will he allow his only daughter to be cast out?"

"Why do you ask? To test me?"

Herodias gave a brittle laugh. "You're clever. Of course to test you. To see whether your ambition is only a spark—or a fire that can again bring greatness to Herod's throne."

"It's been a fire since the night I first looked upon you," he answered. His voice grew lower. "Follow me to Capri."

"Of course I will. We'll plead your cause before Tiberius together."

"Then there remains just one more formality, Herodias."

"To tell Philip I'm leaving him? Oh, no. For years I've longed to stun him with just such a shock. Let him awaken one morning to find that he has nothing left. Not even me."

"Did you think I meant Philip? Be damned to him! When I spoke of a formality, I meant quite a different thing. Formal in the sense that it binds like a pact. Far from formal in actual fact. Come here—"

From behind the hanging came carnal sounds and laughter of that ugly rutting, but it was enough. I crept away from the antechamber and ran to my father's office, where I sat huddled, fighting back tears of grief and revulsion.

Finally I went back to the peristyle and concealed myself. I waited until well past the ninth hour. At last Antipas emerged, muffled in his cloak. He vanished up the staircase to the second story. A moment later I flung aside the hangings to confront my mother.

She was warming herself at her small enameled stove, the last trace of personal luxury remaining in her room. Her hair hung in damp strands. Her cheeks were red. One shoulder was exposed where she had not bothered to fasten up her clothing. On her flesh I saw bruises.

I had expected her to complain about the intrusion. Instead, she smiled. In that smile glimmered the image of a woman I remembered dimly from my childhood, the image of a mother who had loved me, long before ambition and envy and greed had worked their changes upon her. For a moment, though, her face was almost kind.

"Come in, Salome. We must talk. From your expression I suspect you know what happened here this afternoon."

"I heard part of it. I'm not ashamed that I listened. You're the one who should be shamed—cuckolding my father—"

"I love Antipas. He's a great man. Or he will be, when he regains the crown of the Herods. Does it mean nothing to you that I'm a woman who wants a better life for her daughter?"

"You weren't thinking of me when you agreed to run away."

"I was! You're the flesh of my flesh. Whatever life I make in this world will be your inheritance. These past years your father has given me nothing—no affection, not even simple politeness sometimes. He's lived for one thing—his business."

"Any man would seek escape if he were nagged

91

night and day about being a poor provider. Was it his fault he was born a foreigner? Was it his fault he could only become a citizen late in life? That's the real reason you detest him—he's never been able to get you invitations to the noble houses—"

"Perhaps," she shrugged. The gentleness was replaced by a sterner look. "It's really pointless to argue. At last I've met a man who refuses to sit beside the road musing on his own insufficiency. A man who sees a great city ahead, and intends to reach it at any cost. You may find my interest in him deplorable, but at least I'm being honest about it."

"You dare call it honest when you tumble in another man's bed and plan to desert your lawful husband without so much as a word of warning?"

Herodias stretched out her hand, strangely desperate.

"Salome, don't ruin things! Come with us to Capri. You're my only child—"

"My father's child too. I intend to tell him what you plan."

That stung her. She lost all pretentions of friendliness.

"If you speak one word to Herod Philip you'll regret it."

"I've listened to your evil tongue long enough," I cried, turning to run.

She caught my arm and tried to drag me back. I writhed and twisted and at last broke free, plunging through the hangings. She followed me to the antechamber, crying:

"I warn you, Salome. If you value the life of

that young physician, say nothing. *Salome! Listen to me! Salome!*"

Her scream echoed through the house as I ran back to my chamber and called for Gemma. She appeared in a moment, not needing to be told that the interview had failed. She wrung her hands as I burrowed into my one remaining trunk and pressed a goatskin purse into her trembling fingers.

"This is all the money I have left, Gemma. Take it and hire as many street boys as you can find. Describe my father and send them looking for him in the wineshops. Save a little though. Promise it to the one who locates him. Hurry!"

A moment after she had gone off into the gathering winter's dark, I was frightened by a new thought. In my overwrought state I had neglected to tell Gemma that my mother might try to prevent her going, and that she must use great care.

Only then did my mother's warning about Marcus fully penetrate my mind.

Perhaps her words were not just threats spoken in anger—

No, that was inconceivable. She could not be such a monster as to stoop to having Marcus harmed. I could believe many things of her, but not that.

I rushed about the house searching for Gemma but she had already vanished. My mother's quarters were empty too, although lights burned on the staircase leading to the rooms belonging to Antipas. If Herodias were there with him, refining her vile scheme to run away, I didn't want to know. I crept back to my cubicle and blew out the light, huddling down next to the brazier to await Gemma's return.

She came back in an hour, but the task of locating my father proved more difficult than I had anticipated. A full night passed with no results. The following day and night also brought no word from the hired boys. I slept fitfully through that tense time while revelers hallooed up and down the streets outside.

In the murky dawn of the second day, one of the urchins knocked at the front gate. He had located a man resembling my father at the inn of a Greek known as Dion, in a disreputable quarter down by the Timber. Gemma paid the boy the extra reward, and despite her protests I set out through the streets alone. A single woman was safer at Saturnalia than one traveling with her slave. However, in the customary turnabout, the mistress might be forced by a roistering mob to commit all sorts of indecencies at the whim of her servant. With Gemma's wool cloak about my head and shoulders, I appeared to be a slave myself.

A chill mist was fading from the sky under the weak glow of the winter sun as I made my way down to the Tiber. On every street drunken celebrants danced and cavorted. Men and women fondled one another openly. Many wore carved masks. Others carried crudely painted phalli, or long poles with frayed purple banners intended to deride the nobility. Pipes and timbrels beat a raucous accompaniment. I loathed the sight of it all. The carnality reminded me of my mother and Antipas.

The inn of Dion was a tumbledown place in the worst stews of the city. I found my father seated

94

at a table with his head resting upon his arms. The only other patrons of the inn were a pair of Phoenician sailors too drunk to do me harm.

My father's forehead was filthy with dirt and crusted blood from a cut doubtless acquired in some street brawl. His garments were specked with offal and stained with wine. He snored loudly.

Tears sprang to my eyes as I touched his arm and spoke his name.

"No money," he muttered. "Let me sleep, I have no more money—let me sleep."

I shook him. "Father, please wake up."

He raised his head. His eyes were bloodshot, his cheeks unshaven. His lips hung slack. I caught a whiff of his breath, foul with wine. For a moment there seemed to be no brain behind those dull eyes. Then recognition returned. I pulled up a stool and sat down, putting my hand over his. He jerked away.

"What do you want of me, Salome? I've done all I can for you. Oh, yes," he added bitterly, "you've done well by me."

"Father, listen, It's about Mother. She plans—"

Abruptly he jumped up. His face hovered over mine, baleful.

"Stupid girl," he said thickly. "I don't want to hear about your mother."

"But I'm trying to help prevent—"

"I'll have none of your help! Your *help* cost me the life of the Libyan—not to mention every denarius I had to my name."

"I accept the blame for what happened at the Circus! I thought—"

"That is not woman's position, to think. I made

95

my great error in life by assuming horses were somehow inferior to women." He wagged a dirty finger beneath my nose. "I was wrong. Ah, the gods attest to it—how wrong I was. Get away from me, Salome. I don't want to see your face. It reminds me of that whore who bore you."

He began to push me toward the inn door. I struggled and pleaded. His voice became a shriek:

"Get out—*get out!* I wish you'd died in the Circus instead the Libyan, you brainless bitch!"

Chapter II

Bondage

He reeled past me out the door. I ran after him. A crowd of revelers was approaching. I found myself entangled among them.

Hands plucked at my flesh. Voices called lewd remarks as I sought to get away. When at last the group had gone stumbling by, I was alone in the shadow of a grimy apartment building. The thoroughfare was empty, my father gone.

For a time I wandered up and down the nearby streets, overwhelmed by the bitterness of the cup that had come to me. It seemed as though nothing in my world was stable any longer.

Then I remembered Marcus.

How long I walked that day, over rough roads into the countryside under the paling winter sun, I have no notion. I recall that my mind held but one thought, one name—his name. Only he could relieve the terrible gloom of my spirit.

At last I toiled up the lonely hillside above the deserted practice track of the Blues. I was chilled by the wind. My feet were bruised and dirty. I stopped and let out a cry of dismay. The stables were deserted.

The emptiness was clear indication of the financial disaster which had overtaken the company. I searched through two of the buildings before I found another human being—a sickly youth forking hay into a stall occupied by a sway-back mare no longer fit to race.

"Where might I find the company physician Marcus Catullus, boy?"

"In the barracks, I expect. That is, if he hasn't gone yet."

"Gone? Where? To the provinces? To another circus?"

The youth snickered. "Into the provinces? I suppose you could say that. But not to a circus. He's going with the legions. He's no longer a free man. You'd better hurry if you intend to give him the comfort he's hired you for. The soldiers should be here any time to fetch him."

I ran from the stable and stumbled up the hill. The first of the barracks buildings was empty, its few pieces of crude furniture smashed, its cupboards looted by the vanished men who had once served the Blues so loyally.

Crying Marcus' name, I hurried into the next

building. It too was deserted. Where was he? Had he already gone?

Tears salty on my cheeks, I rushed outside and collided with someone. I closed my eyes and screamed. The next thing I knew, my head lay against Marcus' shoulder as he sat beside me on the steps of the building.

The chilly wind rippled the grass that had overgrown the empty track at the foot of the hill. Marcus drew away, his face sorrowful.

"How did you get here?"

"On foot, Marcus. I had to find you."

"Why? You couldn't have chosen a worse time. I'd hoped to go—" he averted his head "—without seeing you and bringing you shame."

"The boy in the stables—he said you were no longer free."

"He spoke the truth. This morning I received notification that my status as a freedman had been revoked by my former owner." He looked bitter. "But he didn't want me back in his service. Instead, I've been conscripted into the legions. Each legion has a slave as its doctor, you know."

"Couldn't you run away?"

"With my parents subject to instant revocation of their freedom too?"

"But why, Marcus? Why did your owner strike out at you?" I dreaded asking that, and yet I knew I must. I saw an ugly pattern emerging, a pattern for which the hand of my mother worked the loom.

"I don't know," Marcus said. "Perhaps my owner was bribed. Perhaps Caligula never forgives an insult. I'll probably never know the answer. But I know this much about Roman society. Almost everyone can be reached. Anyone will do a favor when the purse is fat enough."

That was the moment I guessed the answer. Now I saw the truth! I had paid a price for daring to go to my father—to warn him. I was sure my mother had gotten a purse to the owner of the man I loved. Perhaps Antipas himself had provided the money. The terrible irony was that I had lost Marcus and my father both.

"Marcus, I think I know how this came about."

Surprised, he said, "How?"

"I caused it."

"Nonsense! *You?* What could you have to do with the misfortunes of an insignificant doctor?"

Slowly, I told him of the succession of events which had led to this meeting on a lonesome hill far from Rome. The winter sun was a cold eye gazing upon us. The shadows lengthened. Marcus listened with an expression of disbelief as I finished.

"So you see, this is my mother's revenge—"

He shook his head. "I can't believe it, Salome. But it makes no difference. The result is that we'll never see each other again."

"Never see . . . ? But surely—"

"The Empire is huge, my darling. And slaves in the legion are never set free."

He touched my cheek, his eyes lighted by love and a sadness almost to great to be borne.

"The daylight's almost gone, Salome. They'll come for me before nightfall. Before I leave—I've no right to ask it of you, but I want to remember you—but I *must* remember you, wherever they

100

send me to die. If we had a single moment to-gether—"

Tears streaming down my cheeks, I pressed against him, feeling the strength of him against my breasts as I flung my arms about his neck.

"Yes, beloved. While there's still time—"

Had I been married at the age a girl customarily marries in Rome, I would have known what it was like—to lie with a man. As it was, I trembled when Marcus drew me into the dim barracks. He spread his rough cloak and embraced me.

His hands were gentle, touching me almost shyly at first. But when he held my breasts and kissed me, I felt a strange, uncontrollable yearning in my body. There was brief pain, soaring ecstasy—and finally a tender lassitude more beautiful than anything I had ever known.

His lips were soft against the curve of my neck. He covered my nakedness with his cloak to protect me from the wind whistling through the ruins of the barracks. He stroked my hair, and I had never known such sadness.

"I'll love you no matter where I go, Salome. Know that. Remember it."

"Oh, Marcus—we'll see each other—"

"Yes, of course," he said with a resigned smile. "In the next world—if there is one. Still, I feel better now. I could die tomorrow and know that I've shared a glory even the wealth of Tiberius couldn't buy."

"Marcus, I promise to find a way to buy your freedom—"

"Hallo! We seek Marcus Catullus. *Physician, where are you?*"

Marcus scrambled up. "The soldiers!"

Quickly he pulled his cloak around him, gathered up his little kit of medicines, and leaned over me for a final kiss. His lips tasted sweet. Yet the kiss was lonely as death.

"Goodbye, my darling," he whispered. "May the gods treat you well."

Then he was gone.

I crept to the door, my gown clasped to my breast. In the somber light of late afternoon the helmets and breastplates of the four soldiers who had come for him gleamed dully. One of the men spied me and laughed.

"Saying farewell to your strumpet, eh, physician?"

"Shut your mouth or I'll shut it for you," Marcus snarled.

"Ho!" exclaimed the legionnaire. "Fancy you can act like a gentleman of exalted station do you? We'll soon correct that notion—"

He pulled his sword and gave Marcus the flat of the blade across the temple.

Marcus sprawled in the grass. His eyes were hateful. Then he must have remembered the terrible burden he bore—the responsibility for his parents. He clambered to his feet, as the soldier gigged him in the small of the back with the point of the sword.

"March, doctor. We'll teach you humility in the legions, you can count on that."

Numbed by the cold, I stood in the doorway watching the group move down the hill. Marcus climbed into a chariot behind one of the soldiers. Soon the party was out of sight beyond the poplar grove where my love had given me the gift of the silken veils.

The wind whistled through the deserted buildings. Too frozen and empty to cry, I went to fetch the rest of my clothes.

Listlessly I wandered out of the barracks and directed my steps back in the direction of Rome, knowing I did not possess the courage to take my own life, even though the prospect seemed attractive.

It was then, as I rounded the corner of the last stable building, that I saw the other chariot.

The sickly stable youth was talking with its driver, who now dismissed him with a wave. I couldn't believe my eyes. In a heavy woolen mantle, his cat on his shoulder and his oiled skull gleaming, by the light of the dying sun, there stood Thoth the Alexandrine.

"I've come to drive you back to the house of your mother, Mistress."

"How—how did you find me?"

"I have ways."

"You filthy creature!"

I leaped into the chariot and dug my nails into his throat. He was surprisingly strong. He flung me off. His tiny eyes gleamed.

"There's no point in struggling, Mistress. You're going with your mother. To Capri. Then to the palace of the new King of the Jews. You will live well, your mother promises you that. She wishes you at her side. Come, Mistress, climb up. Your life in Rome is finished. Even Gem—"

"*Gemma?* What about her?"

"There was a most unfortunate accident. She was killed in the streets only a few hours ago. A drunken carnival crowd fell upon her without warning only a few hours ago. She was raped several times before she died."

"Arranged by you, no doubt."

He never so much as blinked.

"I have no idea what you mean. Climb up! We've delayed too long already. With all due respect, I think you know who is master now."

He continued to stare at me for a long moment. *"I tell you, climb up."*

Grief-stricken and drained of will, I bowed my head and took my place behind him.

Marcus was not the only one helpless in bondage.

Chapter III

Capri

The rabble of Rome called the island where Tiberius had built his twelve great villas Caprineum, the place of the goats, after the lewd, goatish ways of the aging Emperor.

On the road overland to the shimmering blue bay where the island nestled beneath the ominous loom of Vesuvius, the smoking mountain, we heard many a traveler publicly refer to the Emperor by the name Biberius Claudius Nero—in other words, the drinker of straight wine. Clearly I was journeying with my mother, Thoth, Antipas, and his retinue, to a place where immorality was not only tolerated but encouraged.

Our house in Rome had been auctioned. Since my last meeting with my father in the shabby tavern by the Tiber, I had not laid eyes on him. Nor had I heard a word about Marcus. With the laying away of the body of my faithful Gemma, the final stone in the wall between myself and the old, settled life had been mortared into place.

I had reached the conclusion that decency gained a person little in the modern world. Everyone lived by the standards set by the old man who dwelled on Capri—standards which my mother and Antipas, fondling one another like lovers even on public roads, had adopted as their own.

I still cried in the dark of the night, when I thought of Marcus. But by day I tried to harden myself for our visit to Villa Io, where Tiberius was currently residing.

The curved bay, surrounded by bursting green hills responding to the warmth of the southern spring, sparkled and reflected the silvery sky as a small vessel bore our party across the water to the cliffs. Only one dock was available, swarming with Praetorians. Antipas pointed out that having one dock made it easier for Sejanus to control the flow of visitors.

Tiberius had certainly been a great man in his time, the first to successfully enforce the peace of Rome throughout the Empire, and the first to collect taxes on a profitable basis as well. But it was common knowledge that as he had grown older, his appetites had become more depraved and he had relinquished most of his power to Sejanus, who now virtually ruled the Empire from this island. Sejanus was a low-born soldier who had risen high by means of his wits.

As we ascended the cliffs toward Villa Io, shining white in the sun, there seemed to be much open criticism from the slaves about this powerful minister, not to mention remarks about the Emporer's perverted tastes. I got the idea that Villa Io must be a cesspool of wicked behavior, and rather than being sickened by the information, I found myself shivering with anticipation.

That reaction made me realize how far I had fallen. But only a fool would scruple over the immorality of Capri. After all, didn't the Emporer sanction everything that went on? I would make the ways of Capri my ways, and try to forget.

Climbing steadily up the cliffs, we passed the oak tree which, according to the legend, had been dead and twisted until Emperor Caesar Augustus set his foot upon the island. Thereupon the tree had burst into leaf, and Augustus had decided to construct a dozen villas here to be the playground of Emperors. Villa Io was the most beautiful of the lot, with immense marble doors and intricate mosaic floors, scarlet and yellow walls, endless grottoes and gardens and shadowy retreats where all manner of sin was practiced.

Within a day we fell into the rhythm of life on the island. Antipas met with various functionaries to arrange his audience with Tiberius. There were so many persons ahead of him that it appeared it would be weeks before he could be presented.

Since he and my mother Herodia were constantly occupied with private conversations concerning the future of the kingdom of the Herods, I was left to myself a good deal, surrounded by slaves and treated to every luxury the vast apartment put at my disposal could afford.

I soon discovered that Capri swarmed with rascals and opportunists of every type. There were Greek astrologers vying with one another to cast the Emperor's horoscope; poets eager to win favor by reciting the laudatory odes; and fortune hunters by the score. These last were mostly perfumed young fops who hoped to attach themselves to older courtiers and thereby win a legacy.

Every last client was given the sportula, a daily basket of food or its equivalent in coin. With such extravagance, it was no wonder the coffers of Rome were said to be depleted in spite of the zeal of Tiberius in collecting taxes.

Praetorians could be seen everywhere, not to mention whole troupes of men and women, trained since youth to perform carnal acts in public. These lewd players were the favorite entertainers of the Emperor when he was not cavorting with his minnows—little boys he took into his bath—or poring over his personal copies of the famed love treatises of Egypt, the Elephantine Books.

At a small dinner to which our party was invited, I watched a bit of the performance of the troupe, but I soon sickened of it and retired to my chamber. I felt ashamed of my own hypocrisy—a stocky, handsome young Praetorian was waiting for me in my apartment, and I let him take his pleasure with me all night long. He had not been the first, nor the second, since my arrival.

What right had I to condemn the pleasures of

Tiberius? I asked myself. None at all. Yet when I held the Praetorian in my arms through the moonless night, I received no satisfaction, even though he was an expert lover. As he gasped out his passion I felt a dreadful ache within me, and I called the name of Marcus aloud.

The Praetorian became angry—his name happened to be Vitellus—and only another surrender on my part would calm his rage. I obliged him without argument. He was a body to fill a void that was not physical alone, a void that could not be filled, except by one man.

At last, Antipas gave enough purses to enough people to gain his audience. I was not allowed to be present for it, although I gathered it was a success when my mother rushed into my chambers to inform me that Tiberius had been well pleased with the report on the activites of Pontius Pilate. The Emperor had scheduled a ceremonial dinner at which I was to dance.

"You must be beautiful for the old man, dear," Herodias said, patting my arm. "He's fond of young girls. We must take care to display you well and make sure he sees enough to please his appetite."

"Never fear," I sighed, glancing over her shoulder at Thoth standing near the entrance. "I'm sure you and the Alexandrine will see to everything, to suit your own plans."

My mother threw me a curious glance. "I find you changed, Salome. More pliant. You used to fight at every step."

I mocked her.

"Do you really find that so strange?"

"I do. The gods work in mysterious ways," Herodias murmured piously.

"So do eunuchs from Alexandria," I returned.

The barb did not bother Thoth. Whatever strange desires drove the obsequious half-man to serve as my mother's agent had lifted him to a positon of eminence. He was resplendent in a new tunic and gold sandals, and smiled blandly at me, his cat on his shoulder like a demon out of the underworld.

But the slave dealers who had castrated him in Egypt had unleashed a terrible force. This was clear every time he laid his eyes upon me. I knew he could not possibly want me. And yet, because of the glint in his eye, I sometimes wondered—

"Whatever you wish of me, Mother," I said, "I'll do. I've thrown my lot with you now. I promise to dance well."

Herodias walked about me in a circle, smiling in satisfaction. "That's good to hear. I've also heard that you're quite popular with certain of the Praetorians. Your figure has grown fuller, too. So the tales must be true? You have found ways to amuse yourself here on Capri?"

"Are you shocked?"

"Why should I be shocked by a girl taking a lover?" She patted my cheek. "Just be careful, Salome. Don't get yourself with child by some lout like that ridiculous physician you fancied in Rome. You're destined for better things."

"I should have guessed you'd have a practical reason for the warning."

She was oblivious to the sarcasm. Her eyes shone and her cheeks were flushed with excitement.

110

"There is a regal house waiting for us across the Great Sea, Salome. A house in which a new king will be crowned soon. That future is too promising to throw away. Every action we take, every word we speak here on Capri, must be directed to one end—securing the kingship for Antipas. When it's his own, it's ours as well. I'll be queen. That title can be yours, one day."

"My thanks for such a precious gift," I said, turning away quickly so that she wouldn't see the tears springing into my eyes.

Six nights later, before hundreds of clients and slaves, in the great formal atrium of Villa Io, I danced before Tiberius Claudius Nero the Younger, Emperor of all the provinces of Rome.

I danced in a pale saffron stola of such thinness that my body was clearly visible to all who watched—especially the Emperor. I danced the dance of maid and god with considerably more variation, to excite those who watched.

Tiberius was an old man. He reclined in a stupor upon the highest couch in the torchlit atrium. His purple toga was slimy with the grease of a suckling. He presented a fearful sight, but not because he was tearful himself. To the contrary, he was hoary and thin, and smelled vile.

But on his lips and cheeks and chin, running sores shone in the gleam of lamps and torches. At other places upon his scrawny arms and neck he bore white scars where hot irons had burned away the lesions. Marcus had once told me the sores came from a disease Tiberius had contracted as a result of sleeping promiscuously with unclean women. Whatever the cause, he was a

111

ghastly sight, and all the more so because he was supposed to be the most powerful man in the Empire.

He regarded me with a blank face while I danced. As though to flaunt his indifference, he fondled a naked boy of seven or eight who lay simpering beside his couch.

On one side of him sat my mother Herodias and Antipas. They laughed and drank, totally oblivious to the indecencies Tiberius was committing on the person of the boy.

At his other hand, lying rigid on his elbow, was Sejanus, the black-jowled counselor whose gaze seemed even more lifeless than that of his master. While the coldness of Tiberius angered me, that of Sejanus frightened me.

This was the man who had banished four thousand Jews from Rome, deploying them in the legions on a useless mission in Sardinia until they all sickened and died of fever. This was the man who had shipped statues of himself to Judea to inflame the populace and remind them of his authority. Even as I scrutinized him, I suspected his mind was busy, perhaps deciding which undesirable citizen would next feel his wrath, in the form of his favorite torture. Vitellus had described it. A supposed traitor was forced to drink wine in volume, after which a cord was wrapped about his genitals until he died in agony.

The timbrels beat their throbbing rhythm. My feet flew across the mosaic floor. My nakedness seemed horrible all at once. I was performing like some street wanton before these evil, lustful people. I had not become as hard as I liked to pretend.

112

Mercifully, the dance soon came to an end.

Cries of approval rose from the couches. I bowed my head, then raised it, astonished to find a vacant smile of pleasure on the Emperor's face. He crooked a finger to beckon me to his side.

I found myself incapable of movement, horrified by the rotted look of the Emperor's flesh.

Sejanus raised himself on his elbow, as if to ask who I was to ignore an imperial summons. The odors of roasted flesh and wine sickened me suddenly. This was an evil place, and it was wrong for me to be part of it.

Chapter IV

Nefer's Fury

Frantically, my mother signaled with her eyes. I remembered I had nowhere to run, no one to give me sanctuary. Resistance disappeared. The bracelet of tiny silver bells on my ankle tinkled as I approached the royal couch. At least he had sent the little boy packing off.

The old man extended a fire-scarred hand that shook with palsy. I made obeisance and tried to keep from gagging at the stench of the sores. Even pots of incense held by slaves could not mask the smell.

His cracked lips widened, but what emerged was more a cackle than a laugh.

"A fine and skilled daughter you have raised, Herodias."

My mother's eyes shone unnaturally bright. "It is to the credit of the Emperor that she is a true Roman girl, sire. Under the Emperor's wise rule there has been peace—and the opportunity to school the child well. If there were one strong arm to uphold the Imperial eagles in the Jewish provinces, the Emperor's peace might be extended and perpetuated there, too."

Sejanus snickered openly. It was all too clear to him that Herodias was brazenly flattering the old man. Tiberius, however, merely blinked his watery eyes and gestured in a vague way.

"Ordinarily, of course, we could not sanction this alliance of yours. Both you and Antipas are charming people. But each has a spouse. To flout the law by going off together to your fortress at Machaerus might only stoke the fury of the rabblerousers. Sejanus has borne out your story, Antipas, that these Jewish sectarians are fanatics when it comes to the rules set down by their god."

"Their god is an abomination," Sejanus spat. "This Yahweh they worship is supposedly all gods in one. His very existence is an insult. The Jews must be taught that there are no gods but those of Rome!"

"Then a strong central authority is the only logical answer," said Antipas.

"The crown of the Herods can't be given willynilly to the first tetrarch who begs for it." Sejanus retorted.

115

"I would never beg before any man!" Antipas began. My mother seized his arm.

Amused, Sejanus waved a wheedling finger at Antipas.

"But that isn't to say that the dog who smells meat at the end of an alley won't eventually close his teeth on it. It all depends on how well he fights his way through the other dogs barring his path. A firm hand—no, let me amend that—a *ruthless* hand, a hand that crushes the Jews into the earth—might prove to be the hand that could hold the royal mace of Herod the Great. But only *afterward*, you see. Afterward, then there is proof of strength."

"I agree. Oh, definitely," Tiberius muttered. His eyes rolled as he searched for his little playmate. Finally he saw the child crouching behind a pillar wolfing a butt of bread.

He gestured him to his side. I hastily resumed my place on a couch near my mother. Sejanus spoke again.

"The Emperor has raised a valid point, Antipas. Casting off a legal spouse is the sort of act that could stir up a great deal of trouble among the Jews. If you then deal harshly, you will have a minimum of public sentiment on your side."

"But my wife belongs to a barbarian tribe."

Sejanus threw an accusing finger at Herodias. "Her husband doesn't."

"He deserted me," Herodias said. "I can find a hundred witnesses."

Sejanus chuckled. "I think the Emperor has found a clever servant, dear lady. I'm sure that your ambition will more than make up for what-

116

ever laxness there has previously been in enforcing the law in Perea and Galilee."

"Any law can be bent to order," murmured the Emperor vacantly, "if the higher law of Rome is served thereby."

"And if the Jewish scum are wiped out before they start a full-scale war," said Sejanus. "Deal harshly with them, Antipas. You'll be rewarded. Perhaps even with the reward you crave most."

"Death is the only proper reward for those who defy the Empire," my mother declared. Her breasts rose and fell beneath her gown in a manner that showed me she was greatly aroused. "The Jews should be chained, and if that isn't enough, killed outright!"

Sejanus touched the Emperor's arm. "I think Imperial rule in the provinces is beginning to take a turn for the better."

The old man nodded drunkenly, running his hand through the ringlets of the child at his feet. I wondered how much longer we would be forced to remain at the banquet. Already it was growing undisciplined. Couples at the far end of the hall fondled one another and shrieked for wine. Tiberius waved.

"Go to Perea, Antipas. Take the lady with you. Don't fret about the law for the time being. I say she is yours by right."

"The Emperor won't regret his decision," Antipas said.

"Then seal it with the grape."

The old man raised a goblet into which slaves hastily poured wine and honey from silver jars.

"And strike up the music so Villa Io rings with merriment—to celebrate the return of order."

117

Tottering to his feet he cried, "The lyre! Pluck it loudly! The——"

Without warning he pitched forward on his face.

Bowls and goblets flew helter-skelter. Sejanus leaped up. Herodias uttered a cry. But on examination it proved that Tiberius had merely drunken himself into a state of dizziness. He lay sprawled across the table, stoney eyed and drooling.

Slaves rushed forward with basins and cloths. Tiberius rolled over upon his belly and began to vomit upon the dining table.

I thought the banquet would end, but it had only begun. Tiberius recovered, shrilled for more wine, and the drinking began in earnest, with all manner of debauchery taking place in plain sight. I seized a cup of wine and began drinking as fast as possible to dull my senses. Tiberius, having refused a change of clothing, gulped draught after draught, cackling gleefully at the spectacle of men and women writhing on the couches in the torchlight.

My mother and Antipas seemed to be enjoying themselves immensely, but my head ached from the noise. When Tiberius tottered to his feet, shrieking for attention, I turned away hurriedly, running for my apartment before I became ill. Behind me, echoing down long corridors I heard his voice cry out to his guests:

"After me—oh gods, after me—let fire destroy the earth."

Sick and sobbing in the darkness, I was not so sure that it would not come to pass.

And soon.

In the early summer when sea travel became safe, our sojourn on Capri came to a welcome end.

I said goodbye to the Praetorians with whom I had tried unsuccessfully to dull the memory of Marcus. We took ship. The great trireme beat southward in an unruffled sea, passing through the Messina strait, and then took a course for Alexandria with the favorable northwesterly winds behind us.

I was alone a good deal on the voyage, but I preferred it that way. My mother, Antipas, and Thoth were a constant trio under the great awning, where the tetrarch explained in detail the various political and religious problems confronting him. I did little more than study a crude map of the country in question, for I expected it to be a hot, desolate place.

Once we had cleared the mighty lighthouse at Alexandria and sailed northward again to our landfall at the swarming port of Sidon, I saw that my supposition had been correct.

The port was crowded with strange, hooded desert men, dark of face, with strong features and black eyes, descendants of the Idumaeans whose blood I carried in my own body. As they labored to unload our baggage, I heard none of the soft refinements of Rome in their singsong speech. Only when we were borne overland on a good Roman road, with a tribune and legionnaires to guard us, did I hear again cultured Greek.

Jews were everywhere, for they were forced by law to carry the goods of any Roman citizen one stadia. Through long days in the littor on the sweltering road, and through equally long nights in crowded noisy caravansaries, their ritual cry—"shalom!"—rang constantly in my ears.

The sun shone down so fiercely in Galilee that I had little inclination to look at the landscape, which was generally arid, relieved only here and there by pomegranate bushes or groves of olive trees. We passed eastward, and then to the south, along the shore of the Sea of Galilee where the sails of fishing boats bobbed. From there on we followed the tortuous valley of the river Jordan until, at the end of a seemingly endless journey, we neared the northern end of the brackish Sea of Judgment.

Our destination was Machaerus, an ancient Idumaean fortress on a pinnacle overlooking the Dead Sea. From this fortress Antipas governed his provinces, and the closer we came to it, the more imperious my mother became with the slaves and soldiers—all except Thoth, of course. He had even been provided with his own open litter and a parasol.

We forded the Jordan near a place called Bethabara. Antipas sent a tribune ahead to Marchaerus to inform his wife Nefer that he expected her to be gone with all her followers upon our arrival.

The roads turned into little more than foot trails as we bore upward through steep mountains. Below, the Sea of Judgment spread out north and south, seething with gray, poisonous mist. Beneath its surface, said the Jews, the ancient cities of Sodom and Gomorrah had sunk when Yahweh cursed them for their wickedness.

That this was a wicked land I could well believe, but for a different reason—it was harsh, forbidding, and stern, in sharp contrast to the few green vales we had passed at scattered points along the Jordan. Machaerus itself reared up at last beyond the river Arnon, a maze of towers and walls hewn out of solid basalt by Herod the Great.

I glanced from the litter as I was borne to the huge gate and felt a shudder in my spine. Distantly a patch of green glimmered at the Bethabara fort far in the north. All else was savage rock. Legionnaires prowled the towers, and the fetid mist floated far below.

Unpleasant news awaited us. The tribune whom Antipas had sent ahead came running up, exclaiming:

"Tetrarch, your wife Nefer is still inside the fortress."

Antipas' face darkened. "Then you'll suffer for your bungling."

"Tetrarch, she plans to leave. In fact, her followers have already packed and gone down the mountain. But she wishes a word with you first."

"Whatever she wants to say, it can only be spiteful," Herodias said. "Nefer knows she's beaten."

But my mother's confidence hardly prepared us for the spectacle awaiting us in the high gloomy hall of the fortress.

Like some savage animal of the desert, lithe and dark, Nefer stood alone, resplendent in a cloak decorated with the feathers of peacocks. Her strong brown arms blazed with primitive bangles. Her hair shone like ebony. She was still a young woman, fair of body, and she held herself with a pride that many a Roman senator's wife would envy. When she spoke, quietly, it was in fluent Greek.

"I had to wait, husband, if only to lay eyes upon the woman who has cast me out."

Antipas strode forward angrily. "Be off, Nefer! You only make things more difficult by your presence here."

"I belong here! I am your lawful wife, and this is my rightful home."

"No longer," he replied. "Your home is eastward, in the tents of your father Aretas. Return to him and I'll send a generous settlement—"

Nefer pointed accusingly at Herodias. "Can all the wealth in your Empire wipe out the perfumed stink of this harlot you've brought into my house?"

My mother tried to remain cool, but there was a raw reek of hatred between the two women that no amount of civility could conceal. Nefer turned to me.

"The woman's daughter is a harlot as well, for being party to this vile scheme. I won't be cast off by such creatures."

"My patience is short," Antipas said. "Tribune! Take her from my sight!"

Booted feet hammered. Legionnaires closed in around Nefer.

She was borne bodily from the chamber, shrieking like the wild child of the desert that she was.

"Mark me well, Antipas. My father will bring blood on all your heads for this insult. He'll sweep out of the desert to destroy you—and your harlots too!"

There was no mistaking her intent. She felt me equally as guilty as the woman who had actually claimed the tetrarch from her. I shuddered with relief when at last she was gone from the hall.

Chapter V

Proposal

In the days that followed I tried to take an interest in the politics and customs of the land which my mother was coming to look upon as her personal domain. But I had difficulty talking with the servants—most of them Jews who knew no Greek—and there were no girls of my own age, among them.

Antipas proclaimed Herodias his wife, although they had not bothered with a Roman ceremony, nor even sacrificed to the gods to appease them. Shortly after this, my mother persuaded Antipas to dismiss nearly all the Jews who performed menial tasks in the vast, empty fortress. Thoth became chief steward, wearing a chain and bronze medallion inscribed with Idumaean characters to denote his new station. His only rival for authority was a wizened little Jew named Chuza, who had charge of Antipas' vast vineyards. Chuza knew so much about the native soil and culture that Antipas could not afford to get rid of him. But otherwise he cleaned his household of those he described as potential troublemakers, and lost no time dispatching a courier to report this to Sejanus. Then he and my mother set out on a month's journey around his domain.

I did not accompany them. But scarcely a week after they had gone, I had a series of erotic dreams about Marcus.

One morning after a particularly bad dream, I sat down in the garden under the looming fortress wall to straighten my mind on the subject.

Wasn't Marcus as good as dead? Why couldn't I free my mind of him? I hit upon the answer. Almost daily I wore one of the seven veils he had given me, as a girdle about my waist. Perhaps I should stop worshipping these scraps of silks and treat them as if they had no special significance.

Accordingly, I began to use the veils for a purpose for which they were never intended. I employed them during the long hours in which I practiced my dances, moving and swaying silently in the stillness of my quarters. I fashioned the dances to be symbolic acts of love, and I soon found I could twist the veils about my loins and breasts with little feeling for what they had once symbolized.

Yet beneath my satisfaction at breaking their curious spell lay a heartache I could never quite suppress.

The tedium of life in the fortress was relieved shortly after Antipas and my mother returned. They were flushed with enthusiasm for their crusade to wipe out the dagger-carrying Sicarii. Antipas had no sooner ordered several of his tribunes into the territories to enforce strict curfews upon the roads, than word came of the impending arrival of his half-brother Philip the Tetrarch.

Coming to Machaerus, we had passed through Bethsaida, the tiny fishing village on the Sea of Galilee from which Philip governed the provinces of Trachonitis and Iturea. But the Tetrarch had been on a journey to the north at the time.

He came bearing gifts of enamelware and spice—valuable gifts but not ostentatious ones—and he seemed not a bit perturbed when Herodias received them without much interest. Philip did not so much as lift one of his white eyebrows at the sight of Antipas with a new mate by his side.

At the formal banquet which Antipas gave, I danced for our guest. He was a slender man and a very old man. He moved slowly, clad in simple peasant robes which my mother privately said were unbefitting a tetrarch. His skin was the color of the cedarwood of Lebanon, for he had lived many years in this sunny part of the Empire. He seemed to possess great politeness and restraint, and I soon found he had other admirable traits as well. This came about when I chanced across him in the garden the evening after the banquet.

Seeing me approach, he turned and smiled, extending his veined hand.

"My child. I bid you greeting."

"And I greet you also, Tetrarch. I didn't mean to disturb your thoughts."

He waved. "I've been thinking about Nefer's departure. I mean no disrespect to your mother, Salome, but to incur the wrath of Aretas of Nabatea is dangerous. He is a fierce king, and could marshal thousands of desert tribesmen should he decide to avenge the insult to his daughter."

"Then you don't approve of the new alliance?"

A thoughtful look crossed his face. "No. Do you?"

"What my mother does isn't my concern," I shrugged. "I have no power over her."

"But she has power over you, doesn't she?" he said, speaking Greek more fluently than I had heard many a scholarly man speak it in Rome. "Come, sit down with me a moment and let me ask you another question."

There was a strange, almost tremulous look on his wrinkled face as he led me to a grotto carved into the basalt wall of the fortress. There, in the thickening purple shadows of the night, on earth damp with the mists off the Sea of Judgment, he clasped both my hands between his.

"I find you a lovely young woman, Salome," he said at length.

"I thank the tetrarch for his flattery."

"It's not flattery. It's the truth. You're far too young and vital to be left to languish within the walls of Machaerus. Let your mother scheme with

Antipas—" Here he smiled again, tolerantly. "I'm too old to envy what they fancy is their power. They told me about the favor they gained with Sejanus and the Emperor, but I've seen provincial officials come and go in my nearly seventy years, and there's one lesson I've learned—power turns to dust the moment the breath whistles from the lungs."

Bewildered, I said, "That's true enough, Tetrach—"

"Please call me Philip."

"Very well, Philip. But I don't understand what concerns you?"

"Simply this, my dear. Herodias has no right to hide you within these gloomy walls. For one thing, there are men in the dungeons who aren't fit for human eyes to see."

I shivered. "I've heard their screaming late at night."

"The air is foul here, Salome. In Bethsaida it is fresher. There is always a lovely golden light in my garden."

Now I began to sense his intent. He leaned forward, his thin face pale as a statue's in the waxing moonlight. I shook my head.

"If you mean what I think you do, Philip, I don't want to seem ungrateful—"

"The boon would fall on me alone," he broke in. "I'm old. My health is poor. You could bring both beauty and youth into my modest home. And I could spend what little time I have left without loneliness." He brushed idly at an insect. "Today I have nothing—no one. I waited too long, my dear. I hope to rectify the error."

"I couldn't accept your proposal, Philip. We hardly know one another—"

The aging Tetrarch chuckled. "My child, I'm no young swain smitten with passion. In fact that's the only reason I thought it might be unwise to speak to you. Trees wither. Where their branches once turned green in the spring, in the winter they are lifeless. I couldn't offer you—that, but I could offer everything else to—"

"We are related by blood," I said hastily, growing apprehensive about his quiet determination. "Roman law forbids marriage between ascendants and descendants. We would be violating—"

"But I tell you I am quite incapable of physical passions. Dear child, understand that I propose marriage only because it would get you out of this dismal place, make you secure when I die—and endow you with what little wealth I've accumulated."

"You have a way of turning a girl's head, Tetrarch," I laughed softly. "It would be a pleasure to escape from this fortress."

"I would be kind to you," he said, and my heart almost broke.

"You've already been more than kind. But I can't accept. I'm not sure I could be a suitable wife to any man. Too much bitterness has come my way."

"In the sunlight at Bethsaida, scars would heal."

I leaned forward to touch his cheek, feeling neither bold nor fearful now, but somehow safe and free to speak my mind. "If only I could repay you for making me feel wanted again. A moment ago I was ready to offer myself for your pleasure. I can't do that now. To demean your kindness with a cheap promise of—"

"Ah, Salome, don't speak so bitterly. Love should be joyous. It's the birthright of the race, and the hallmark of great feeling between man and woman."

"That's why I didn't offer, Philip, I don't love you—I doubt if I ever could. Forgive me for being cruel, but I can be no less than truthful with you, since you've been the same."

"It's the difference in our ages," he said wearily. "But I swear you would be happy at my side. There'd be no difficulty over leaving. Last night after the banquet I spoke to Herodias. She seemed in favor of such an arrangement—"

With a low cry of dismay I leaped up.

"Salome, I didn't mean to alarm you. Please—"

Hot tears scalded my eyes. "I can't do it." Turning, I hurried away. "I can't, Tetrarch—I can't marry you—now or ever."

Sobbing, I fled to my quarters. I saw hateful visions of my mother conspiring with Antipas to marry me to Philip for the gods knew what reason, and the more I thought of her hand in the affair, the more I rebelled.

For a moment Philip had swayed me with his promise of escape. Had I been given free choice I might well have accepted. But with my mother having a part in the business, never.

During the remaining days of Philip's visit, we conversed several times about the literature and art and the peculiar religious beliefs of the Jews, but no personal matters were raised. He seemed withdrawn. When the time came for his departure he held my hand briefly.

"May your days here be bearable," he said, so that my mother, who was standing nearby, could not hear. "Perhaps we'll yet be friends."

"Tetrarch, we'll always be friends. I'm sorry that I can't offer more—"

He shook his head. "I understand your feelings and I accept them—although leaving you behind in this dreadful place nearly breaks my heart."

He kissed my cheek in a chaste way, then whispered, "Thank you, my dear, for your candor—and for a moment of warmth."

He climbed stiffly into his litter, assisted by his slaves. As the caravan started down the rocky slopes I said a prayer asking whatever gods he lived by to grant him some happiness during the rest of his life.

When Antipas stalked away and began bawling orders to the legionnaires about the courtyard, my mother approached and took my arm.

"Did you find the company of the tetrarch pleasant, Salome?"

Wary, I said only, "His visit broke the monotony."

"I know this life is not a comfortable one for you, even though we're much better off then wo were in your father's house in Rome. But believe me, Salome, in the days to come there will be splendors in this fortress of a kind not seen since the days of the great Herod. Meantime, perhaps we should do something to get you out of this somber setting. I confess it even palls on me."

I wanted no favors from her:

"I'm quite content. I have no desire to leave."

"Not even for a visit to Jerusalem?"

"Herod's capital city? I thought you meant—"

"What, Salome? What was it you thought I meant?"

Deep in her eyes she was laughing at me, sensing my antagonism.

"Nothing, Mother."

"Antipas plans to pay a state visit to Pontius Pilate. In fact, he's making arrangements for the cisiums to be ready at the foot of the mountain at dawn tomorrow. Would you accompany us? I still think a change of scene might do you good."

"All right, I'll go," I said, trying not to show my eagerness to be away from this hideous pile of stone. She fell to chattering with me over the various sights we would see in the famed city where Herod had built a great temple for the Jews. I was so excited that I did not stop to question whether this might be merely another of her devious plans whose purpose I could not guess.

Chapter VI

A Doctor in Fortress Antonia

My spirits light for the first time in weeks, I set out with them next morning. Even the presence of Thoth riding ostentatiously in the last of the four cisiums did not disturb me.

A small company of legionnaires under the command of a tribune marched ahead. The light, open carriages were comfortable enough, for we raised paper parasols over them, and the soldiers were present in numbers sufficient to frighten off lurking bands of Sicarii. We made rapid progress. After three nights spent in silken pavilions which the soldiers erected for our comfort, we arrived at the ford of the Jordan near Bethabara.

The region was an ugly one, all sharp hills and tumbled black boulders. Only a few thin sycamores provided shade. We paused to water the horses. Antipas strode back to the carriage in which my mother and I were riding. He pointed to a nearby hill overlooking the sycamores. Nature had carved a depression from the black rock.

"That's the pulpit I told you about, Herodias. From there the Essene spews out his traitorous pronouncements against Rome."

Contemptuous, my mother drew her palla tighter around her perfumed shoulders.

"Do you suppose if I brayed like a wild ass he'd appear? Didn't you tell me he's a savage? Eating nothing but honey and dead locusts pressed into cakes?"

"Some nauseating stuff of that sort," Antipas nodded. "He must be away, or he'd certainly show himself. He always shouts at the legions when they pass by."

"I don't know this man," I said. "Who is he?"

Antipas spat in the dust. "A wandering preacher. He calls himself John the Essene, after the sect to which he belongs. He runs about in a camel's-hair robe and schedules his sermons so he can preach when the hot springs beneath these rocks belch steam. It frightens the Jews out of their wits when he starts talking of Yahweh."

"Surely no one listens to such a man seriously," my mother said.

"That's just the trouble," Antipas growled. "They do. Next to the Sicarii he's the most dangerous influence in the province. Sooner or later he's going to have to be dealt with, before he baptizes too many of the Jews into the service of that abominable god of theirs. If he were here now, I should probably have the tribune haul him back to Machaerus in chains."

"How can you put a man in prison for speaking his mind?" I asked.

My mother flung me a withering glance. "You understand nothing of the local politics, Salome."

"I understand that even in the Forum, men can criticize Tiberius."

"*Be silent!*" Herodias exclaimed.

"But you don't sound very enthusiastic when you threaten to have him chained, Antipas," I persisted.

"Well, the Essene does tend the sick hereabouts. At least he relieves the government of that burden."

"Anyone who speaks against Rome must be destroyed," Herodias exclaimed. "Never forget that, Antipas—or the fact that Sejanus expects achievement from you, not just promises."

Antipas threw her a look I can only describe as one of loathing. Perhaps he too was getting his fill of her reckless ways. She smiled at him, a slow sensual smile. Like a mask slipping into place, his expression became resigned.

A shout from the tribune informed us the horses were rested. Antipas walked up the line to his cisium. My mother preened herself and rearranged her palla. I began to see that for all his boasting, Antipas would have remained an ineffectual governor had it not been for her influence.

A few days later we reached Jerusalem. The city, seen at first as no more than a shine of gold

135

from the roof of the great temple, proved to be a maze of narrow streets and twisted passages in which half the unwashed population of the world seemed to mill. Cries of merchants hawking their wares assailed us as we bumped through the street in closed litters, Antipas deeming it prudent not to flaunt himself in an open cisium. Consequently my first view of Jerusalem was from a window of Fortress Antonia, the Roman stronghold built at one corner of the sprawling Temple.

From there I could gaze down on the innumerable courtyards leading into the Holy of Holies where, I was told, a non-Jew would be slain if found. The noisiest of all the courts was the outer one, the Court of the Gentiles, which was crowded with Romans and Jews alike. They all jostled one another amid the bleats and coos of sacrificial lambs and doves. A fearful stink rose from that swarming mass of unwashed humanity, and I was grateful when a servant summoned me to the noon meal in the apartment of the Roman procurator Pontius Pilate and his wife Claudia Procula.

A short time in the procurator's presence— with my mother fawning and smiling over him so that you would think he was Antipas' friend— disenchanted me about an extended stay in this crowded city.

Pilate was a short, colorless man, well educated to judge from his speech, but somehow lacking firmness. He described his troubles to Herodias and Antipas as though he had no idea they considered him an obstacle to the throne of Herod. And his troubles seemed to be legion.

First there were the Sicarii. These, he asserted, swarmed through the streets of Jerusalem and held secret meetings to inflame the populace against Rome.

The voice of John the Essene reached Jerusalem as well, proclaiming that the many gods of Rome would one day be overthrown by a messiah.

Finally, a new source of concern had been added in the person of a Jewish carpenter, a man by the name of Jesus, from a town called Nazareth. He was apparently going about Judea working what the populace referred to as miracles, and was even rumored to be the son of Yahweh himself. Pilate dismissed him as a crafty politician trained in Egyptian medical arts which bewildered the local people.

At this point Herodias began to sympathize with Pilate. Once or twice she threw the procurator a glance whose meaning was unmistakable, a glance offering far more than friendship. Antipas kept Pilate's wife in conversation so that she was not aware of the byplay. The entire proceedings sickened me so that I could eat little. After formal introductions no one had paid me the slightest attention, so I managed to slip away without difficulty. I preferred the stinking Temple courtyards to the intrigue-laden air in Pilate's apartment.

Drawing my palla about me, I went from the Fortress to the Court of the Gentiles, and from there to the Royal Porch, roofed with Lebanon cedar. Under it, bearded rabbis intoned the Jewish law to groups of the faithful. It was while I was half-listening to the unintelligible speech of one of these aged teachers that I saw a familiar figure crossing the court from Fortress Antonia.

For a moment I thought sunlight had played a cruel trick, shining as it was from the helmet of the soldier striding through the crowd. I looked again.

"Marcus!"

He turned and saw me. Then, to my astonishment, he walked on.

I fought my way through the crowd and threw my arms around Marcus. Tears streamed down my face. Many Jews turned their heads in disapproval, though I no longer cared. I rested my cheek against Marcus' breastplate.

"Beloved—the gods have been kind. If this is the end of the earth to which they've sent you, then it was a blessing when I came with my mother to the end of the earth too."

Roughly he pushed me away. His face was harsh.

"Leave me alone, Salome. Forget me."

"Forget you! When I've only found you again after months and months—?"

"I hoped against hope this wouldn't happen. I didn't think the gods would play so cruel a trick. In a few more hours the legions would have been gone—"

Astonishment overwhelmed me. "You sound as if you knew I'd come to Jerusalem—"

Gazing out over the crowd he said stiffly, "I've said too much already."

"Marcus—beloved—we've just begun to speak to one another—"

He whirled on me. "I told you to forget me! Remember, I'm a slave. Physician of the

138

Fifth Imperial Legion in Judea, nothing more. I'm a cipher—a dead man. And I won't make love to a woman promised to another."

"Promised? *By whom?* Marcus, I don't understand—"

"It's useless to pretend, Salome. I've lost the feeling I had for you."

"That's a lie. I can see by your face—"

"You're to marry Philip the Tetrarch," he interrupted. "I've been told all about it. I'd sooner walk away now than go through hell trying to forget you again."

He threw his scarlet cloak over his shoulder, turned, and vanished into the noisy crowd.

Chapter VII

Stalemate

"Which one of you told Marcus Catullus I was to marry Philip?"

I spoke the words harshly. All through the afternoon I had roamed the streets near the Temple, searching for Marcus without success. Then I had returned to Fortress Antonia. The centurion on duty at headquarters of the Fifth Legion had claimed not to know Marcus' whereabouts. He said only that he had gone into the city in search of herbs and ointments for his medical chest.

From there I went straight to the chambers of

my mother where I found her with Thoth. I confronted them with my question but if I had expected a startled reaction to my question, I was disappointed.

My mother had been painting her eyes with kohl while the Alexandrine stood by stroking the cat on his shoulder, his bald skull turned shiny by the reflected light in the sky above the Valley of the Kidron. Both turned to stare at me, their faces impassive.

"It won't do any good to lie," I said. *"Who told Marcus?"*

"Of whom is she speaking, Lady?" Thoth asked my mother. "Surely not the young physician she fancied in Rome."

"That's the only Marcus I'm familiar with," Herodias shrugged.

"Stop giving me those blank looks! If we're to be enemies, at least let's be open about it."

My mother feigned a hurt expression. "How can you accuse me of being your enemy? I have only your interests at heart—and the interest of our family."

"Was it in my interest that you had Marcus informed I was to marry another man?"

"Dear, I'm afraid your words are utterly confusing—"

Thoth raised a ringed hand. "Wait, Lady. Perhaps it serves no purpose to carry on this pretense. Clearly your daughter knows of what she speaks. It might be wiser to bring things into the open."

Herodias bit her lips and then laid down the mirror she had been holding.

141

"Very well, Salome. I had hoped to prevent an open breach, Salome, but you force it upon us."

I laughed in her face. "I, Mother? It's you and this—who have been managing everything behind the scenes. The day you brought this Alexandrine into our house, you ruined our life."

Herodias stiffened. "I'll hear no word against Thoth."

"Why not? I'm sure it was his idea to tell Marcus that lie."

Her eyes grew hard. "No, Salome, it was mine."

Trembling, I said, "Did you also arrange for Marcus' freedom to be revoked back in Rome?"

Instantly Herodias became evasive. "I don't know what you're talking about."

"Liars! Both of you! *Abominable liars!*"

One of Thoth's ringed hands slashed out, striking me and sending me sprawling. Herodias seized his arm and pulled him back.

"No more!"

I struggled to my feet. "I'm finished with you, Mother. This time I mean what I say."

Her laugh frightened me. "Do you? Where will you go? Into the streets? I fancy that a few hours wandering about in the filth and squalor of this town will bring you back. You're not a woman—you're little more than a child."

"I'm sixteen now, Mother. When I find Marcus I'll stay with him. I'll be free of you—"

"Be silent!" She leaped up, fury in her eyes. "You'll do no such thing! I intend for you to marry Philip."

"You see, Mistress," Thoth purred, "it was no lie I told the physician."

"You admit it, then!"

"Of course he admits it," Herodias said. "I planned it for your benefit—to prevent exactly the sort of unpleasantness that has occurred."

She became wheedling again.

"Before we left Rome, I sent Thoth to make inquiries about Marcus' assignment in the legions. I knew the largest overseas detachments were stationed in this country, and that there was a chance you might encounter him. Only a chance, mind you—but as I feared, it happened. When we arrived in Jerusalem, I sent Thoth to find the physician and warn him against any hope of reunion. Otherwise he might have started trouble. I'm sure he heard the tetrarch of Galilee and Perea was paying a formal visit to the procurator."

"You had no right to take matters into your own hands!" I cried.

"But it's for your own good, Salome! You could never marry Marcus. He's a slave."

"So you want to arrange for me to marry Philip instead?"

"Since you press me on the matter—yes."

"Well, I won't do it. Nothing can force—"

This time it was my mother's own hand, heavy with rings, that stung my face.

Wonderingly I put my fingers to my cheek and felt warm blood. Herodias stalked back and forth, breathing rapidly, her words biting.

"My patience is wearing thin, Salome. If I compel you to marry him you'll do it. There are sound reasons for the match."

"But I don't love him! I could never love such an old man, not in—"

143

"How naive you are! Don't you realize Philip is sickly? By his own admission, he can't live much longer. If you are his wife when he dies, it would further solidify the claim of Antipas to the crown of the Herods."

I stared at her for a long moment and saw at last the full, shameless depths of her ambition.

"Surely the crown of the Herods can't be so valuable that you'd do anything to get it, Mother. No woman could want power that much."

"You don't think so? Had you lived as I did for years—seeing every penny wasted on a racing company, watching important people snub us—perhaps you'd understand. A person born in the gutter seldom aspires to power. The prize is too far away. But living as we did on the fringes of the nobility—only tolerated, never accepted—you see how close the prize is. Just a short step. One day I'll go back to Rome as a queen—and the fine senators' wives who rebuffed me will grovel."

"No matter what price you pay?"

"No matter what price I pay," she repeated. "But perhaps you still don't believe I'm serious. Perhaps that's why you fight me at every turn. So let me tell you something else."

I shook my head and tried to turn away. "I've heard enough—"

She seized my arm. *"You'll listen!* Do you know what I did last night? I went to the chambers of the procurator. I gave myself to Pilate so we'll have one less enemy to worry about in the months to come."

"After you cuckolded Father, you cuckolded Antipas too?"

144

"Stupid girl! Antipas knew all about it. We planned it. Together!"

"Stop this!" I shrieked, covering my ears. "I can't listen to such filth—"

"But you can!" She tore my hands away and held me so tightly, I was forced to stare into her dark eyes.

"Pilate and I now have a little understanding over disputes that might arise between our provinces. He thinks that a temporary willingness to give in to Antipas' demands could mean richer rewards in the future—rewards he's already sampled. Antipas knows about the arrangement, but publicly he'll pretend otherwise. One day when there's an important test of power, I'll be able to sway Pilate—and make Antipas look all the better in Rome. So you see how serious I am. I've staked my life on the crown of Herod—and I'll stake yours as well."

"Let go," I said quietly. A strange fearful calm had come over me. "There's no need to treat me like an animal."

"You're behaving like one."

"I won't anymore. You and Antipas may do whatever you wish but I draw the line at marrying Philip. Nothing will force me to be his wife."

"Not even if the marriage could bring his part of the Empire into your hands?"

"Not even then."

"Then it seems we're temporarily stalemated."

"Call it whatever you wish."

"Don't forget there are ways of breaking a stalemate."

Thoth had turned to the window and was fondling his cat. His shaven head was outlined

145

against scarlet clouds above the Bethany Gate and the Kidron beyond.

"But I'm forewarned, Mother. That in itself is protection against your plots."

She twisted her enameled nails in the folds of her gown and regarded me with naked hatred.

"If I decide you are to marry Philip—" She stopped, then said more softly, "But please don't force me to such a test of wills, Salome."

"It's only your ambition that will force it."

"But remember this. You have nothing to match the strength of that ambition."

Her arrow struck home. What resources did I have? None. The ties of security, comfort, and most of all, the primitive tie of blood bound me to her even in moments like this. Thoth had turned and was staring at me with one of his strange, oblique gazes that mingled contempt with another emotion I did not want to understand. I straightened my gown and faced my mother, trying to hide my own feelings of vulnerability.

"You tell me I have no strength, Mother. Time will tell."

So saying, I left her.

She might very well be speaking the truth when she said I could never marry Marcus. Yet slaves had escaped their masters before. In Jerusalem, far from Rome, few would care if we ran off together and made our way to another city to begin life again.

Night had fallen by the time I returned to the quarters of the Fifth Legion. An old Jew woman, her back bent by years of work, was sweeping the corridors with a broom made of rushes. In the afternoon, when I had sought out the tribune, the halls had rung with noisy talk. Now there was only silence, punctuated by the swish of the broom.

"Old woman," I said in Greek, hoping she would understand, "I'm looking for a physician attached to the Fifth Legion."

"The Fifth Legion has marched," she replied, her Greek broken but passable.

"When?"

"At sunset. This time of year, they move out to drill and put on a show of strength in the provinces."

"Where did they go?"

She lifted one shoulder, expressively. "Who knows? If your business is important, you'd best hire a courier to go after him. The roads aren't safe these days—especially for pretty Roman ladies."

Heartsick, I turned away. I remembered something Marcus had said—he had known about the imminent departure of his legion. For a moment I entertained thoughts of pursuing him, but I discarded them. In the confusion of Fortress Antonia, with a great city to surround us, we might have had a chance to escape and go into hiding. In open country, we would have none. It was doubtful whether the commanders of the legion would even allow me to approach Marcus. So my plan was temporarily aborted. My only consolation left was the knowledge that if Marcus was permanently stationed in Jerusalem, I could return to Machaerus, and still flee back to the city if Herodias pressed the issue of marriage.

Somewhere there must be a strength to help me get through this terrible time, I thought. My mother had centered her whole being upon her husband and the power he might one day hold— and in her own bemused way, I supposed she almost worshipped that goal. But I had nothing to worship, nothing from which to draw encouragement, nothing to sustain faith in the future. The god of the Jews was strange to me. And the gods of Rome, I was sure, could exert little influence this far from the Capitoline. Perhaps if I returned to Machaerus and spent time in solitary meditation, I might order my life and find a source of courage for the troubled days that obviously lay ahead.

Chapter VIII

Daggers on the Highway

But it was not given to me to make the return trip to Machaerus in peace.

We were still a day's journey from the fords of the Jordan when the cisium in which I was riding stopped with a lurch. Up ahead, one of the legionnaires let out a scream.

"Sicarii!"

At once the soldier who had been serving as my driver hauled out his sword and leaped to the ground. I shielded my eyes against the sun and glanced up the road to the source of the shouts and oaths. My heart turned cold.

A dozen men were scrambling down the rocks. Their leader, a lanky, black-bearded man in a filthy tunic, carried a curved dagger in each fist and a third between his teeth.

The legionnaires fumbled with their swords and shields. Before they were ready for the assault, the leader of the zealots raced to the road and plunged his dagger into a soldier's belly.

Herodias scrambled from the cisium ahead of mine and hurried back to huddle beside me. Antipas stood up in his own vehicle, sword drawn, shouting exhortations to his men. The Sicarii, however, fought with the strength of devils. Another soldier dropped screaming. The leader of the band of attackers snatched the eagle standard from its bearer and threw it in the dust.

"Why doesn't Antipas fight?" I exclaimed. "Why does he just stand there flourishing his sword?"

"His life is too valuable to risk in such an encounter," Herodias said, struggling with the reins as the team began to balk. "Our lives may be forfeit too if these savages defeat the soldiers. We must rescue Antipas and flee!"

She maneuvered the cisium out of line, calling commands to the frightened animals in language that would have made a charioteer blush. It was impossible to tell which side was winning the fight. Too much dust had been stirred up. But I suspected the Sicarii were holding their own against the legionnaires who were hampered by their armor.

From his cisium Antipas saw us coming to his rescue. He gestured frantically, urging Herodias to hurry. We were passing the carriage in which she had been riding when a figure suddenly loomed up on the far side of it. The man vaulted to the seat, then leaped from there to our vehicle.

"Shall we come to a stop, ladies?" he said, tearing the reins from my mother's hands.

He crouched before us, teetering on the narrow foot board above the yoke, smelling of sweat, his skin burned brown by the sun. His smirk of victory promised no good.

Without warning, he ripped my mother's palla at the shoulder.

"Fine clothes you wear—but the poor women of Bethany don't even have rags for their infants." A dagger flashed in his hand. "That's what I call injustice—of the Roman variety."

"Mother, I recognize this one. He must be the leader. He came down the hill first."

"And I'll go up the hill last—after I've carved up some Roman flesh. I'm especially anxious to get hold of Antipas. I've waited months to catch him on this road. He spends most of his time cowering behind the walls of Machaerus, sending out his tax edicts. Well, now it's our turn to tax him. We'll start by taking the pound of flesh from you, Lady."

He seized my mother's wrist, dragging her forward so that her throat was a hairsbreadth from his blade. For a terrible moment I hoped he would kill her.

But I couldn't let it happen. I clawed at his throat. He yelped and cuffed me.

"Perhaps I ought to deal with you first, girl!" Then he grinned, wiping off the blood I'd drawn.

"If you were a man, you'd fight with your comrades and wouldn't attack women."

"I attack Rome," he snarled. "And you ladies are Rome itself."

"Then be done with it!" Herodias tore open her bodice, exposing the cleft between her breasts. "Win your splendid victory against a woman!"

The bearded man hesitated. More shouts sounded up the road.

Herodias laughed suddenly, full of contempt. "What are you waiting for! Strike!"

Her bluff worked.

The young Sicarii looked into my eyes. Then with an oath of disgust he leaped to the ground.

"God will punish me for my weakness—but I can't do it. You must be Antipas' harlot, the one John the Essene has preached against. Well, I salute you. You're a brave woman in your own fashion. You saw my weakness and exploited it. I have to spare you—but not your adulterous husband. I bid you good—*what's this?*"

His scruples had undone him. Down the road, the poorly armed attackers had at last been defeated by shields and strong swords. Three of the Sicarii lay dead in the roadway. The rest were scattering up the hillside. One shouted:

"Quickly, Aaron, before they catch you!"

The young man darted around our team, leaped into the vacant cisium, and would have driven off had not the first of the soldiers hurrying up the road seized the halter. Another legionnaire attacked from the other side, delivering a sword cut to the Sicarii's right arm.

The zealot flung his dagger. It clanged harmlessly off a shield. More soldiers closed about him. The young man howled and raged in his native Hebrew while the soldiers dragged him to the ground.

They subdued him with kicks and blows. At last he lay still in the dust, bleeding heavily from his wounded arm.

Pale and out of breath, Antipas arrived just as one of the legionnaires were about to thrust a sword into the Sicarii's stomach.

"Hold!" Antipas panted. "This one gets special treatment. I recognize the long beard and the camel's-hair robe. Haul him to his feet!"

Antipas regained some of his courage, strutting back and forth before his captive. "Aaron of the Caves is his name, Herodias. He's the worst of the lot. We must carry him back to Machaerus and make sure he's given a fine execution—one the local population won't soon forget."

"You'd better do it quickly, Tetrarch," Aaron breathed, "before God himself strikes you for your wicked ways."

"It's this ridiculous god of yours who's causing all the trouble!" Antipas exclaimed. "Until you Jews realize that, the whole countryside will run with blood."

"At least I'm willing to die for my god," Aaron said. "From the way you cowered during the fight, I can't say the same for you."

"I've a good notion to have you gutted where you stand!" Antipas roared.

Herodias raised a hand. "Wait. This man attacked Salome and me. He was about to kill us when the soldiers arrived. I think he needs more than a simple execution. Lash him to one of those sycamores. Let him taste the whip—then walk all the way to Machaerus at the end of a rope collar.

Perhaps those who see him pass will be taught a lesson."

I turned to my mother. "But he wasn't going to kill us. He spared us!"

"Pay no attention to her, Antipas. He had his dagger at my breast."

"Tie him," Antipas ordered. "Flay him until he screams."

The wounded Sicarii was dragged up the hillside to the grove. His hands were tied above his head and the robe ripped from his back. The soldier applying the whip used it so expertly that it stripped flesh from Aaron's body with every stroke.

Each time the whip landed, Aaron of the Caves stiffened, his back arching in pain. He didn't cry out.

When he had received twenty strokes, his head lolled onto his shoulder. Antipas called a halt. But Herodias wanted more. She leaped from the cisium and rushed up the hill, tearing the whip from the soldier's hands.

"Make him scream his treason for all the world to hear," she cried, laying on the whip savagely.

I covered my face, sickened by the sight of blood streaming down the zealot's back. Herodias gave him twelve more strokes.

At the end of that time he had fallen into such a dead faint that nothing could rouse him. Disgusted, my mother flung the whip away and came back to the cisium. Her eyes were glassy; her breasts rose and fell rapidly.

As Antipas ordered the young man cut down, she stalked back and forth. In that instant I realized what I must do.

154

Climbing from the cisium, I searched in the dust for one of the daggers Aaron had dropped during the struggle. When no one was looking I picked it up and hid it in my gown. Antipas bawled orders for the pavilions to be erected for the night.

Guards were stationed in a circle to prevent another attack, should the remaining Sicarii be lurking up in the rocks. There were wide gaps between the men. Herodias disappeared inside her pavilion and I retired to mine, clutching the hidden dagger.

It seemed hours before the swollen red sun sank. I excused myself from the evening meal and settled down for a long wait.

When the stars were shining, the last of the cook fires extinguished, and the lamps blown out in the pavilion of Antipas and my mother, I crept barefoot into the dark. I made my way to the sycamore grove where Aaron of the Caves had been tied in a sitting position so his naked back would rub painfully against the bark.

He gasped when he saw me. I pressed one hand over his mouth. With the other I thrust the knife against the ropes. In a moment he was free.

"Go between those two guards on the hillside," I whispered, pointing. "Creep on hands and knees, and I don't think they'll see you."

"What's your name, girl?"

"Salome."

"Why are you helping me?"

"You spared my life. No more talk! If you get safely away, the guards will think your friends came back. No one will be the wiser."

Swaying a little, he stood up. He touched my hand and smiled in spite of his pain.

"I will ask Yahweh to bring you blessings, Salome."

"Go, Aaron, while there's time."

I watched him until he crept out of sight. The cry of a night bird disturbed the lonely stillness. I threw the dagger in the underbrush as I walked slowly back to my pavilion. I didn't care whether Aaron's angry god could bring me benefit. I only knew that I had struck back at my mother.

It was a small victory, but a satisfying one.

Chapter IX

Prophet in the Wilderness

There was a great uproar at dawn when the young zealot's escape was discovered. Antipas seemed the least disturbed. But my mother fell into a rage, so he sent the soldiers to search the nearby countryside while we breakfasted. They returned as the sun was climbing over the hills to the east, having found nothing.

Washing down his meal with wine in the shade of the awning, Antipas dismissed their failure with a wave of his hand.

"Time enough to haul him in when we take all of them. We really can't risk arousing the wrath of the Jews until we have more troops at our disposal."

"How long do you intend to wait?" Herodias said irritably.

"I've already written Sejanus that we must have one or two extra legions at Machaerus. I'm powerless until he sees fit to grant the request."

"Nonsense. You have soldiers aplenty. You've got them working your vineyards when they should be fighting."

"The vineyards are a source of income."

Exasperated, Herodias glowered at the soldiers lounging over their corncakes in the shade of a sycamore.

"First things first, Antipas. When are you going to grasp that simple fact? If you'd counseled your men properly last night, they wouldn't have been asleep when the Sicarii slipped through the lines to rescue their comrade."

Then she added a sentence that turned me cold. "If indeed the Sicarii did it."

"What foolishness! Who else could have cut him free? I trust my legionnaires."

My mother's glance drifted across mine, then onward to meet that of Antipas.

"You're right, of course. None of the soldiers would be so stupid as to feel sorry for a rebel trying to overthrow the authority of Rome. The Sicarii must have come—silently. But I heard no noise. I slept soundly. Salome—did you rest well last night?"

"Very well, Mother." I only neglected to add that my sound slumber had come after I had set Aaron free. "Perhaps Thoth did the deed."

"I should scold you for such a wicked accusation."

"It's no more wicked than accusing Roman soldiers!"

Herodias sighed. "I suppose not. Antipas, you should take those soldiers from the vineyards and put them back on the roads. Do it as soon as we reach Machaerus, or we'll have a revolution on our hands. When Jews like that Aaron find they can be rescued from the very camp of the tetrarch—"

"The harvest might suffer—" said Antipas doubtfully.

"Which do you covet more? The crown, or a basket of grapes? I pray the gods I haven't made a wrong decision about you."

"No, my dear, of course not. Perhaps we could do with additional detachments on patrol until we get word from Sejanus. I'll see to it instantly when we return." He rushed over and took her hands in his. "Don't think I'm indifferent to your opinions. It's just that I have a great many things to think about—"

My mother smiled warmly, raising her face to be kissed. "I understand. I spoke discourteously. I'm sorry." The point was won.

"Excuse me, please," I said. "I must see to my things before we break camp."

In truth, I had nothing to do while the pavilions were taken down, tied up in packs, and lashed to the backs of asses. But I could not stand to watch my mother drain Antipas of what little strength he possessed.

At our house in Rome, he had shown a spark of initiative, though it was the wrong sort. Now I

159

saw that he was even less of a man than I had thought. I hoped the remainder of the journey would be free of degrading scenes of the kind I'd just witnessed.

My hopes went unfulfilled. At the fords of the Jordan we met even more serious trouble.

The desolate region through which we traveled that morning was a jumble of ugly black rocks. Sulphurous bursts of smoke rose from the underground springs. The road grew crowded with Jews from country villages. The Jews always opened a path for us and caused no trouble. But I was aware of many angry glances, and several people pointed at my mother, who was riding beside Antipas in the foremost cisium. Herodias looked at the rabble along the roadside with open contempt.

We forded the Jordan when the sun was directly overhead. As the cisiums rattled up the bank, I saw a startling sight ahead. A lean figure with arms upraised was etched against the sky in the rock pulpit which I had observed on our journey down to Jerusalem. A hundred or more Jews had gathered below the pulpit blinking in the acrid smoke which rose about them. They nevertheless stood still listening attentively to the Jewish preacher.

On orders from Antipas the legionnaires drew their swords. The mules plodded forward at a slow pace. The Essene lowered his arms and stopped talking. Singly at first, then in large numbers, his listeners turned to look at us as we rode past.

On the rocky promontory, this John the Essene made me shiver. Truly he resembled the fearsome

160

Yahweh as I had imagined him—lean, tanned to a nut color, with wild unshorn locks and beard. He wore a hairshirt belted about the loins.

He turned his blazing eyes upon Antipas and my mother. For a moment it seemed we would be allowed to travel on without interruption. Then the preacher's powerful voice rang out.

"Hold, Tetrarch. Listen to the voice of God."

As though my mother had coached him, Antipas brought the cisium to a halt and stood up, pointing an accusing finger.

"And you hold also, Essene, or you're liable to get an iron collar around your neck. Who are you to give orders to a representative of Rome?"

"I am the representative of the most high God."

"Your God is a small, meaningless deity in the Roman pantheon. His presence is allowed only by the grace of Emperor Tiberius. Don't forget that, my friend."

"I am not your friend," returned John in a voice whose vigor was surprising for one so old. "I am your enemy, Herod Antipas. You bring false gods into our land."

"Permit me to continue my journey," Antipas answered, with considerable mockery. Herodias dug her fingers into his arm, nearly beside herself at John's effrontery. Antipas continued:

"I don't care to be lectured about your queer Essene beliefs. You may shout and tear your hair all you want, so long as you remember that our patience is not inexhaustible."

"My beliefs are simple as black and white—the white of Yahweh's teaching and the black, godless ways of Rome."

161

"Be careful," Antipas warned. "You're close to treason."

"I am close to truth!"

"If you incur the displeasure of Rome, your god will be driven from these hills and you'll never see his face again."

"Do you imagine we need graven idols to see our God, Tetrarch? He is here, even in this place—for all the world's His handiwork. He cannot be locked up nor scourged with whips. I am His voice, Tetrarch. Prophesying in the wilderness your downfall by His hand."

"Arrest him, Antipas!" my mother cried. The soldiers stirred nervously, awaiting orders.

"And risk the wrath of this mob?" Antipas whispered. "Don't be a fool."

For once he had made a wise decision. There were many ugly expressions on the faces of the Jews clustered beneath the basalt pulpit. The slightest spark could cause a riot that might end with the Jews overwhelming us. Not that I would blame them too much. The behavior of Antipas was insufferable.

"I counsel you to preach your lunacy no more, Essene."

"Who are you to counsel me, Tetrarch? You, who sit before us resplendent in your sin? Reveling in the open display of your adultery?"

"Silence him!" Herodias shrieked.

"No human voice can silence God Almighty!" John thundered. He flung out an accusing finger. "You, woman—you are a harlot! You, Tetrarch—you are an adulterer! The story is common knowledge from Capernaum to Hebron—an abomination in the ears of the Lord. I demand that you cast off the harlot and return to the ways of righteousness before Yehweh takes vengeance. It is not lawful for you to possess her!"

"March on," Antipas cried, nearly strangled with anger. He collapsed on the seat of the cisium, and began punching the carriage driver. "Get started, you churl!"

Herodias tore at his sleeve. "No. Turn back! Order the soldiers to kill him!"

Antipas struck her across the face. *"Enough!"*

Clearly he was frightened of provoking an incident, for he bawled commands that sent the soldiers trotting up the road. My own cisium started forward with a lurch. Instantly the mob broke ranks and closed in behind it.

From the rock pulpit the voice of John the Essene continued to cry condemnations of my mother and Antipas. The terrified driver of my carriage screamed as a rock hit his shoulder. He lashed the mules.

We escaped just in time. A shower of rocks fell behind us. In the cisium which my mother had vacated to ride with Antipas, Thoth the Alexandrine stood looking back at the pulpit in disgust and rage.

Chapter X

Bride and Prisoner

During the remainder of the journey to
Machaerus we encountered no more difficulty. But
my mother and Antipas quarreled constantly. She
demanded imprisonment and death for the
Essene. Never before had I seen her so furious.

Antipas, his anger roused by her nagging,
countered just as vehemently with the argument
that John was still the most powerful religious
leader among the Jews. To strike against him
might provoke the populace beyond endurance.
He would not risk upsetting the delicate balance

of power in his provinces merely to satisfy my mother's wounded pride.

That didn't settle the dispute though. It raged all the way across the Arnon to the fortress. There, thankfully, I was able to hide in my chambers and shut out the abusive language Herodias heaped upon the man she professed to love.

Curiously, I soon began to take a perverse delight in learning about the political and religious turmoil sweeping the countryside.

The servants willingly kept me informed. Many of them, of mixed Egyptian and Arabic blood— Antipas had dismissed all the Jews save Chuza, his vineyard steward—thought I enjoyed watching the local sect obviously heading for disaster. Little they knew that I felt just the opposite. I had no understanding of the religion of Yahweh, but as long as it represented something my mother opposed, I savored its triumphs.

Apparently John the Essene had been infuriated by my mother's presence on the roadway. I heard that he was preaching almost every day about the immorality of the union. The crowds listening to him grew to mammoth proportions as he hammered away at the theme that the law of God forbade Antipas' possessing another man's wife.

The activity of another religious visionary about whom I'd heard at Pilate's table—the carpenter of Nazareth, Jesus—was arousing the Jews as well.

From all I could gather, the Nazarene was a sort of preacher too, although he professed a milder doctrine than that of the fiery John. Further, he was said to possess miraculous powers.

The slaves scoffed, saying that he had undoubtedly learned a few clever tricks while living as a young man among the sorcerers of Egypt. But their scoffing could not quite erase the wonder in their voices as they told stories of water turned to wine at a village wedding in Cana, or a fisherman called Simon from the town of Bethsaida far to the north. After fishing a full night with no result, Simon was instructed by the Nazarene to cast his nets in daylight, when the fish never struck. When he drew the nets in, he found them overflowing.

All other stories were overshadowed, however, by the testimony of the steward, Chuza. His son had been dying of fever. He had gone to Cana in the desperate hope that the Nazarene might possess some healing secrets other physicians did not have.

The Nazarene had told him to go his way, since his son was alive and recovering. Returning home, Chuza discovered it was so. True or not, the story resulted in Chuza's prompt dismissal from Antipas' service.

There was a rising clamor among the people for the Nazarene to reveal himself as the promised king or Messiah who would lead the Jews from bondage and set up a new kingdom. John the Essene had not yet expressed himself on the subject, but that didn't diminish the enthusiasm of the people for this new leader. All in all, the growing religious ferment presented a real problem to Antipas—and to my mother as well.

Twice I sent messages to Jerusalem in the hope that the Fifth Legion had returned, only to have the courier come back to say the message had been unclaimed. Then, on a gloomy afternoon when thunderheads piled in the sky above the battlements, a slave announced that Philip awaited me in the great hall.

"The tetrarch?" I said, arranging my costume and sitting for a last combing of my hair. "I didn't know he was scheduled to visit us."

"He's been here since yesterday, Lady," the slave girl replied.

A cold hand of dread clutched my heart. "Are you sure?"

"I'm certain. He's scarcely left the side of Antipas and your mother since he arrived. They certainly must have important words to say to one another."

I tried to get hold of myself. My fears were doubtless without foundation. Philip had treated me kindly during his first visit, and it was not polite to avoid him.

But I couldn't overcome a feeling of uneasiness as I descended the great staircase. At its foot, a shadow against the gloomier shadows of a gray afternoon, the old man waited with outstretched hand.

I took his hand and presented my cheek. He drew back with a shake of his head. Something was amiss.

"I can't sue for your affection, Salome, until I explain what I've done."

"My, you look grim," I teased. "What have you done that demands such a long face?"

"You're a dear child," he sighed, seating himself beside me on a stone bench. "And a brave one, to put on a show of smiling when I think you

167

already know what I have to say. Plainly I come before you with mingled emotions. Joy on the one hand, dissatisfaction with myself on the other. I *know* I've betrayed you. But believe me—"

He leaned forward suddenly. Tears gleamed in his old eyes.

"I'm frightened of death coming upon me when I'm alone."

My heart was growing heavier every instant. I could barely whisper loud enough to say, "Tell me, Philip. I won't be angry with you."

He turned away. "I've asked Antipas and your mother for your hand."

"It does me great honor to have you do so, Philip," I said, trying to be gentle. It was not fitting for me to vent my anger and fear on a kind old man. "Have you—agreed upon the marriage terms with them?"

"I have."

"Of course my mother was in favor."

"Fully. Not Antipas at first. But Herodias is very persuasive."

"There seems to be nothing she can't get for herself," I agreed somberly.

"Salome, I beg you, don't think too badly of me. But I was sick with longing from the moment I left Machaerus the last time. I promise I'll leave you to your own devices. Never—never touch you, if only you'll care for me in the little time I have remaining. I wanted to approach you first. I only went to Antipas to sound him out. Your mother would hardly let me away from her side until the bargain was sealed. I—but what else can I say? I've made you see me as a doddering old fool."

He lifted his wrinkled face. His eyes shone.

"But I have gained a great prize in the bargain. I—I'm sorry, Salome."

"Don't be," I said wearily. "You're a man, just as I'm a woman. We both have feelings. How can I begrudge you yours?"

"Yet you don't love me—"

"No, Philip. I can't lie about that."

"Nor would I want you to lie. Still, I think we can be happy."

"Can we?"

I thought of my mother's hand behind the scenes, manipulating actors and effects as though Philip and I were characters in a Roman play. Clearly he didn't understand all the hidden currents which were whirling and eddying beneath the surface of events. I sighed and touched his cheek.

"The bargain is truly closed?"

He nodded. "We have made all the arrangements."

"And I have no choice in the matter any longer?"

I had said too much. His eyes brimmed with tears. Thunder rumbled above the ramparts of Machaerus.

"I swear I'll make you a good husband. I'll bring nothing but happiness into your life so long as it's in my power to do so. When I die you'll inherit handsome holdings. A younger man can invigorate them. They'll soon produce the kind of riches I once took from them before I grew too weak to manage them well."

"When is the marriage?"

"There's no great hurry about that, now the

bargain is sealed. Though of course I'm eager to take you back with me to Bethsaida—"

"Thank you for telling me all this in person, Philip."

I turned to go. He tried to follow me. His strength failed him and he fell back, holding out an imploring hand.

"Don't be too angry—"

"With you? No. Philip. But there are others—" The words came thickly. "There are others who—"

It was no use. Tears streamed down my cheeks as I turned my back upon him and fled.

I ran through the empty, echoing corridors of Machaerus where the walls dripped water like the eyes of weeping women. I burst in upon my mother in her chambers, shrieking like a harpy.

"I won't marry Philip. I won't, I won't!"

A heavy hand fastened upon my arm and wrenched, throwing me to the floor.

"You go too far, Mistress."

I lay braced on my palms, staring up at the immense bulk of the Alexandrine. His cat leaped from his shoulder and attacked me, claws unsheathed. Wild with anger, I caught the animal's throat and with a quick twist broke its neck and flung it aside.

I thought the Alexandrine would kill me then. His eyes flared and his hulking shoulders began to shake. He snatched a dagger from his girdle and took a step forward.

"Stop it, before I have you both thrown in the dungeons!"

The scream of anger was my mother's. She

170

flung herself between us and began to push the trembling Alexandrine bodily toward the door.

"Go, Thoth! Stay away until you calm down. It's only a miserable cat. There's far more at stake here than the life of some mangy animal."

She succeeded in forcing him to leave, though his final venomous glance held a promise all too clear. I struggled to my feet just as my mother seized my shoulders, shaking me hard.

"You, arrogant, whining child!"

Crack! Her enameled hand struck my left cheek, snapping my head to the side.

"Vicious, selfish creature!"

Another blow.

"I should have done this months ago!"

A final blow. I stood numb before her, all my strength gone.

"How dare you defy my wishes? I'm your mother, and I demand obedience. You'll marry Philip! Face up to the fact that I can imprison you if you refuse. Now look at me. Say you'll obey."

"I—I—"

The words stuck in my throat.

She slapped me again.

"Say you'll obey!"

"I'll obey."

She dragged me with her to the window embrasure.

"Come here, you spiteful girl. Look below, and you'll see that I have far more serious things to worry about than your childish likes and dislikes. I'll stand for no more interference, not when I'm so close to winning a real victory. Antipas is wavering, but he won't for long. In a week—that man will be dead."

She gestured below. In the shadowed courtyard I saw soldiers leading a bearded figure through the portal that led to the dungeons deep in the rock of the mountain.

It was John the Essene, in chains.

Chapter XI

In the Dungeon

Twenty days after the imprisonment of John the Baptist in the dungeons beneath Machaerus came the fortieth observance of the birthday of Antipas.

Herodias took charge of the occasion, working for days to prepare a feast to surpass any we had ever tasted, even in Rome. The scullery shelves groaned with sausages to be served in porridge, chestnuts and wine and olives and parched peas, young kids and the udders of sows for serving in fish paste. Tiny thrushes had been imported from Sidon, to be cooked with greens, and all manner of seafood as well. The corridors of the fortress began to reek of these delicacies long before the festivity.

The guest list included most of the officers of the Roman garrison, Antipas' vast staff of tax collectors and minor provincial officials, numbering altogether in the hundreds.

As the night of the celebration drew near, the courtyard grew crowded with asses, horses, chariots, and other vehicles.

There was hardly a chamber which did not have all-night dice games or drinking bouts. Herodias deliberately kept the company wholly male, except for herself, so that her preeminence would be apparent. Many of the taxing officers grumbled in private because their wives had not been invited, but my mother had become such a strong power in the tetrarchy that no open complaint was heard.

Fortunately I was spared close association with my mother during this period. After our last angry interview, I had withdrawn even more deeply into my private world, tossing night after night in bad dreams, and waking at dawn to indulge too heavily in the breakfast wine.

In fact, I found wine the only means of enduring the situation.

The servants snickered behind their hands at my disarrayed state when I fell into long periods of wine-sotted musing, but I did not care. The grape eased the torment. It even made it possible for me to listen calmly to my mother's demand that I dance before Antipas and the celebrants as a tribute to my adopted father.

I gave her no argument. Instead I decided I

would make the performance one that Antipas and the guests would never forget. My costume for the dance would be the seven silk veils Marcus had given me—the veils and nothing more.

On the morning of the banquet, I awoke with an aching head and a dry throat. I realized this was because I had been away from the wine jugs scarcely at all during the past two days. I had drunk a good deal as a result of a visit I had made to the dungeons to see the Essene.

What prompted me to go I am not quite sure. Perhaps it was a last ineffectual attempt at rebellion that drove me down the twisting stairs. Far below the earth the damp air smelled of decay. Torches flickered at intervals, lending the scene an eerie look. In the distance I heard the moans of prisoners locked away in some forgotten past, never to see daylight again.

A swollen shadow loomed on the wall. It was a soldier on guard, scowling.

"This is no place for you, Mistress."

"I came to speak with the Essene preacher."

He blinked. "You? Why are you interested in—?"

"Never mind. Just show me the way."

"Your mother will have me whipped if I permit—"

"I thought Antipas was your commander. Isn't he?"

The soldier snickered.

"I order you to answer!"

He scuffed his sandal on the dirt floor. "I don't mean to be disrespectful, Mistress, but—there isn't a man on the post who believes Herod Antipas gives the orders these days. Just a week ago, he came down here to speak with the Essene. When he left he told me there was a possibility we might be releasing him soon. It's risky to hold that Jew, and Antipas knows it. But the very next day, we got an order from the tribune to stop the Essene's daily ration of bread and wine, and—I can't say more."

I stamped my foot. "Finish!"

Nervously, he went on. "Well, the tribune reported Herodias was more eager than ever for the Essene's blood than ever before. She was furious that Antipas even thought about letting him go. The tribune is taking bets that John won't last the week. He wanted me to wager my sagum, but I value a good cloak too much to throw it away on a losing gamble."

"Thank you for telling me all this, soldier."

"Mistress, you must protect me. You mustn't tell anyone where you heard—"

"Stop fretting, I won't. Now take me to the prisoner's cell. If anyone asks why I came down here, tell them I was curious to see whether this preacher was really the fearsome devil everyone says."

"Hardly that," Milus commented, leading me along a narrow corridor where rats scurried, in the dark. "It's my guess you'll find him in his typical posture—yes. I was right. Look."

Drawing back from the grating in the dungeon door, he raised the torch. The bearded Jew was on his knees in a corner of the cell, his hands still clasped in his lap. He rose when the soldier opened the door. There was a serene expression upon his sunburned face.

"I'm honored by a visit from the tetrarch's

adopted daughter. But the guard needn't stand outside. I've neither the strength nor the desire to hurt you."

I gazed and saw he spoke the truth. I dismissed the soldier who marched back to his post after planting the torch in a hook outside the cell door.

"You speak Greek fluently, preacher. I hadn't expected that."

"What did you expect?" John asked, almost smiling. "An unlettered fanatic tearing his hair and gnashing his teeth? Here—be seated."

He dusted a few wisps of straw from the bench which was the cell's only furnishing, and took a seat after I declined his offer.

There was a moment of awkward silence. Then John said: "Yahweh is an angry god when He sees evil, but He's also an understanding god with whom I can talk. Since there are few down here to listen to my prophecies about His anger, I find myself communing with Him often. But if you're seeking amusement, perhaps I can summon some oratorical fire."

"I didn't come to make sport of you," I said.

"Then what was your reason?"

I answered with the truth. "I don't quite know."

A shrewd look came into his eyes. "Perhaps you want to salve your conscience about my coming death?"

"You're not going to die. Antipas wouldn't kill a man as important as you."

"I thank you for the compliment. But I'm well aware of how the wind blows. It's not Antipas who hates me so much as your mother. I've called her harlotry by its rightful name. She can't stand that."

He watched me for a reaction.

All I said was: "If you expect me to be angry, you're mistaken."

He shook his head. "You're a strange young girl. You don't seem at all like your mother. But I'd still like to know why you came here."

"If you must have a reason, let it be this—a question. Why are you set on destroying yourself? You could go free if you'd only learn to live in harmony with Antipas."

"Why should I do that?" he retorted. "We Jews are trodden down beneath Rome's heel and treated like slaves."

"Rome is the power in this part of the world."

"That's where we differ. A man can't serve Him and Tiberius at the same time."

"Why is this Yahweh so much better than the rest of the gods?"

"The rest of the gods are yours, not mine. They aren't even gods, just graven images. There is only one God, and He rules the whole earth, Roman and Jews alike. One day He'll appear on this earth and establish his kingdom. All the legions and chariots and swords of the Empire won't be strong enough to prevail against Him."

"You're speaking of your Messiah?"

"Aye."

"Is it that carpenter, the Nazarene, of whom I've heard?"

"I pray that it is. It's not given to me to know all the ways of God. I only know there is a miraculous healing power in the Nazarene's touch, and he speaks with the tongue of the Almighty. We do

178

differ on some things. His is a doctrine of love and forgiveness. I demand vengeance for sin. But when I baptized him, I thought I saw a divine light in his eyes. Perhaps you would see the same light if you were to meet him. Unfortunately, I doubt I'll be present for such a meeting."

"You seem very calm," I said with some annoyance. "Especially when you face the possibility of death on one of those horrible wooden crosses they use in this country."

John lifted a withered hand in a simple gesture.

"My God gives me strength to face any trial."

"Then I wish I'd made his acquaintance many years ago."

"You can't win His favor in the Roman manner with burnt offerings and the like. You must accept and love Him with your soul if you want to draw on His strength."

"And then he'll wipe away the evil and pain of this world? I don't believe it."

"He can't wipe them away—it's man who creates them. But he makes them bearable."

"Nothing could make this place bearable! Not even your God, preacher."

"Since you believe that, I'm afraid we have nothing more to say to one another."

On that unpleasant note the conversation ended. I left and hurried back along the damp corridors and up the circular stair to my chamber and the surcease of wine. I think I wanted to believe that the Essene possessed the strength I lacked. But my reason denied it. I drank a great deal of the wine resenting—and hating—the Essene more than I had ever hated anyone else.

179

Chapter XII

Seven Veils

In this unhappy state I prepared for the birthday celebration.

I spent hours painting my face and arranging my hair. When night fell, I wrapped the veils tightly about my body, covered myself with a cloak, and descended to the great hall by a rear stairway. I had deliberately begged off from the dinner.

In granting my request, my mother was deceived. She thought I asked because I wished to rest in preparation for my dance, thereby doing even greater honor to Antipas. In truth, I did not go to the dinner because I wanted my first appearance to be a surprise. I wished to shame him by showing his guests what a depraved thing his adopted child had become under his tutelage.

I couldn't help smiling in anticipation. Despite the oppressive heat of the night and the distant mutter of thunder over the Sea of Judgment I felt exhilarated. At the arched entrance to the hall, in the midst of slaves rushing back and forth, I surveyed the gaudy scene before me.

The meal had already been served. I could tell because the hundreds of guests wore rose garlands on their heads—the sign of the start of the heavy drinking.

Pots of incense sent bluish smoke curling to the ceiling. Through the fumes the lolling shapes of legion officers and provincial dignitaries were blurred and misshapen.

But perhaps it was only the wine that made them seem so, I had taken too much, and was not thinking clearly.

A tribune who had been chosen by a cast of the dice to serve as *rex bidendi* was directing the mixing of the latest batch of wine. After this master of the revels passed upon its quality, slaves scurried around to fill cups. From the impatient shouts of the guests, it was apparent that hardly a man in the hall was sober. Drunkest of all was Antipas.

He sat resplendent in his finest pearl-sewn robe, a rose garland hanging crookedly over his forehead. Beside him was Herodias, her face shining, her breasts bared and rouged for the guests to gaze upon. The music of flute and timbrel beat with a steady, intoxicating rhythm.

Herodias saw me waiting. She signaled that I would dance soon. From a passing slave I seized a goblet of wine and drained it.

After a series of seemingly endless toasts to the health and longevity of Antipas, my mother rose and clapped for silence. Quiet spread over the tiers of dining couches, though here or there a drunken guest continued to babble or sing to himself.

"In honor of her father Tetrarch Herod Antipas," my mother announced, "his daughter Salome shall dance for your pleasure."

My cheeks grew hot. How dare she link me so directly to the swollen, sotted creature at her side? Her little speech gave me the last measure of courage I needed. With a flourish I threw aside my cloak and stepped forward to make the ceremonial bow.

Total silence fell. In the distance, the sky rumbled with thunder. A strange blue light flickered in the hall for a moment. On every male I saw sweaty excitement—even on the face of Antipas.

But on my mother's face there was a sudden suspicion.

She leaned forward as though about to stop me. The musicians struck up. It was too late.

Unlike the dances I had learned as a girl in Rome, there was no narrative to this one. It was simply a series of erotic movements. I began slowly. In every pair of eyes I saw doubt. Did they dare express their lustful pleasure over what they were witnessing?

I danced faster. Whirling, I loosened the first of the veils and let it fall from my breasts.

Herodias watched me angrily now, guessing my intent. But I did not stop. I was dizzy with wine, and beyond control.

When the second veil fell Antipas surged from his couch and gave a drunken bellow of approval. Applause and cheers from the guests followed instantly. My mother sank back, relieved.

I threw myself into even wilder movement, suggestive of the most lascivious behavior. But I felt sick. My plot had failed. I was not embarrassing Antipas in the least. I was providing Antipas and his guests with exactly the sort of entertainment their jaded appetites desired.

One by one the veils were cast aside. The pipes shrieked to their final climax. I let the final veil drop, and slumped nude and panting at the foot of Antipas' couch.

Slaves rushed forward with a cloak to cover me. Amid screams of enthusiasm from the guests I rose unsteadily to face the tetrarch.

"Magnificent!" shouted Antipas, waving his wine cup to and fro. The contents splattered over his clothes. "A performance the like of which I've never seem. What do you say, friends? Wasn't it a dance to remember for all time?"

The hysterical shrieking and applause was a mockery, like the smile upon my mother's mouth.

Antipas gestured for silence. He called me forward and stretched out his hand.

"Such skill displayed for our pleasure deserves a reward, Salome. What would you claim in return for the gift of your dance? Name it and you'll have it. Even—"

He glanced dramatically about the hall to emphasize his drunken generosity.

"—even if it's half my kingdom!"

The boast produced another roar of approval, matched by a clap of thunder over the mountains. Blue fire danced outside the windows. In that instant, wine-sotted and humiliated and tormented beyond endurance, I conceived the wicked plan.

"Give me leave to talk with my mother a moment," I said.

"Certainly. Meantime, another round for the guests, master."

I approached Herodias, knowing full well that what I planned was monstrous. Yet I was driven to it by wine, by anguish, and by the knowledge that it might bring my salvation.

"For what shall I ask him, Mother?"

For one heartbeat we were perfectly attuned, our understanding full and complete, like two ferocious beasts who face one another, knowing the moment of confrontation has come.

Herodias smiled, "For the head of the Essene, Salome. On a polished silver charger."

I bent closer so no one could hear my whisper.

"I thought it might be something like that. How badly do you want it?"

Her sly laugh carried her wine-tainted breath to my nostrils. "Why, you're beginning to learn from me. Learn how to get your own way. Daughter—you've changed! Overnight! What do you want in return?"

"I want—I—"

"Go on, daughter. Why do you hesitate?" Her nails dug deep into the flesh of my arm. "Strike the bargain!"

"I want freedom—for Marcus Catullus. Publicly Antipas is Pilate's rival. But privately—you

184

said you had an understanding. Use it. Free Marcus from slavery in the legion—and release me from the marriage with Philip."

"Done!" She threw back her head and shrieked with laughter. "Done!"

"Come, daughter," Antipas called. "Let's hear your request."

Again a hush fell on the hall. Antipas leaned forward, wine dribbling down his chin. I closed my eyes for a second as I approached him. I was taking the last, irrevocable step into darkness. But I saw no other way.

I said without lowering my voice, "Bring the head of John the Baptist into this hall—on a silver plate."

Antipas recoiled as though struck. "Are you mad?"

A shocked murmur ran through the crowd. I stepped close to the tetrarch and whispered:

"Do it. Bring the head to this banquet table—or I'll shame you beyond belief."

About to protest, Antipas glanced at my mother. She met his gaze so sternly that he paled.

Clasping both hands about his cup because they were trembling, he drained the wine, then called two soldiers to his side.

Around the hall several of his sycophants started a chant for the head of the Jew preacher. Soon other, more timid guests began to echo the cry lest they incur Antipas' displeasure. I stumbled to a vacant couch and drank a draught of wine.

Already the enormity of what I'd done was striking through the stupor of my mind. But I seemed powerless to move. Finally I knew I must stop the hideous deed before—

A voice boomed from the archway.

"It is done, Tetrarch."

The tribune stood aside. Two legionnaires marched into the hall. Each held one side of a huge silver charger with delicately engraved edges, meant to carry a whole suckling. I heard groans of horror. Antipas turned whiter still. I bit my knuckle to the bone.

The ashen soldiers bore the charger forward, placing it in a cleared space on the central dining table. One of Antipas' tax officers fainted away. Others retched into their napkins. The hall became so quiet that I could hear the steady drip of blood falling from the edge of the charger to the floor beneath.

And still I could not tear my eyes from the ghastly sight.

The head of the Essene was turned so that its staring eyes were fastened upon me. That gaze, framed by blood-soaked locks, damned me forever.

His mouth had fallen open in astonishment at the moment the sword cleaved his neck. On his face there was no sign of the strength he had prophesied his God would lend him in his hour of trial.

The blood continued to drip steadily, until the table and the tiles were slimy with it. Antipas had turned away. Only Herodias continued to stare at the head. Then she too seemed to have had enough. She lifted a hand.

"Take it out and raise it on a staff in the antechamber, as a warning to all those who defy the will of Rome."

I covered my face with my hands, letting great retching sobs work through my body. I reeled into the shadows behind a pillar and was sick.

I lost track of time. When I recovered and stumbled back into the hall, most of the torches had gone out. The guests, including Antipas, had gone. The storm which had threatened during the banquet had receded. Only occasional flashes of pale blue light illuminated the overturned couches and the litter of half-eaten food. In one flash I saw the ribs of a piglet gleaming like white sticks and a blackish pool still shone beneath the great banquet table.

Herodias was still seated on her couch.

Dimly I recalled the evil compact between us. I had paid too high a price for the freedom of the man I loved. But I meant to claim the reward.

"Herodias—" I called to her across the hall. My voice echoed, so that her name was repeated and repeated in the gloom overhead. "Herodias— *answer me!*"

Slowly, drunkenly, she turned toward me. I dug my nails into my thighs so I would not scream.

"What is it, Salome?"

"You must fulfill your part of the bargain."

"Bargain?" She smiled slowly, dreamily. "Oh, yes."

"A letter must be sent to Pilate. Tonight!"

"No, Salome, I'm afraid I can't do that. I can't upset the delicate balance between this house and that of the procurator—"

"We made a bargain! It's sealed in the blood of that innocent Jew!"

187

Her eyes were oddly bright. "Exactly what did I promise?"

"To free Marcus—and me from the marriage vow."

"Did you believe my words, Salome?"

"Believe—of course I believed them! Mother, in the name of the gods, what evil makes you recant now—?"

She smiled again. "Salome, long ago I told you what I intended to gain for myself during the all too short time that's given us in this life. There is nothing beyond death. I must take what I can while there's breath in my body. If you didn't listen carefully, if you didn't understand that there is nothing I won't do to remove obstacles from my path to the throne of the Herods, you're a worse fool than I imagined. But I thank you for what you gave me tonight. It's the prize I wanted most."

"But you gave your word—"

"Oh, my child! Oh my poor little foolish child."

Her laughter pierced like a dagger. It rang and leaped from the walls until there were a dozen voices of Herodias laughing at me, then a hundred. I covered my ears. Still I heard them.

I began to scream, wordless screams of betrayal and shame. I ran after her as she walked slowly toward the arch, her sandals leaving bloody marks on the floor.

I tried to seize at her garments. She turned on me and gave me a push, loathing my weakness. I slipped and fell.

I tried to crawl after her. Blue lightning burst in at the windows. The eyes of the dead man stared at me like the eyes of his God, bright with the fire of vengeance.

I fell again, my hands slipping in something warm and sticky. When I raised them to my face they were black with blood—the blood left by my mother's sandals.

Then I fell forward and my mind went dark.

BOOK THREE

BEYOND JORDAN

Chapter I

Flight and Sanctuary

An hour after I came to my senses, I fled from Machaerus.

The shrieks and laughter of guests roistering in faraway chambers of the fortress echoed about me like the wailings of the Essene himself, lost in limbo, lost from his god. In my confused state it seemed logical that I could escape my guilt if only I escaped the place where the guilt had been acquired.

I dressed. I took a cloak, the silken veils, and a few denarii, slipped through the watch at the gates and made my way down the mountainside toward the river Arnon in the teeth of a thunderstorm which had erupted suddenly from the wrathful skies.

Blue lightning burst about me. The wind buffeted me this way and that and my clothing soon became soaked. I stumbled again and again, and in a matter of an hour I was exhausted and nearly out of my wits. I was convinced avenging demons were in pursuit, bent on punishing me.

I stumbled at last into a gully, fell over a twisted olive trunk, and dropped to my knees in the rain, sobbing. A chill seized me. I passed gradually into unconsciousness, hearing the voice of my accuser in the wail of the wind. The voice asked why I had committed such a monstrous crime against a god who was not only his god but mine. Finally the exhaustion of the flight down the mountain brought darkness again.

When I awoke, the sun was nearly overhead. Aching and hungry, I clambered to my feet. I drew back suddenly at a clatter of hoofs on the road leading down from the fortress. Peering over the gully's rim, I saw legionnaires in three chariots go thundering past. As they disappeared around a bend, I reflected that Antipas and my mother had discovered my absence.

Instantly I resolved to keep to my original plan and escape them. After a suitable interval to allow the searchers to get ahead of me, I started out down the road. The sky was bright, and the demons that had haunted me during the thunder and lightning seemed unreal.

I still bore a great burden of guilt, but I felt my spirits rise a little with the thought that once

194

I left Machaerus behind, I might escape a little of that guilt.

But I soon discovered I was wrong. By the end of a second footsore day upon the road, I still carried my guilt with me. Alone on a promontory overlooking the misty Sea of Judgment, I wondered whether I should drown myself and wipe out that guilt for which I, and no other, was responsible. Then I laughed bitterly. I could not drown in a brackish sea.

I reviled myself for the laughter. It meant I had committed myself to life. I lacked the courage for death. All I could do was hurry blindly up the road to the north, seeking what, I did not know.

Perhaps I had a dim notion that I could find a haven at the court of Philip in Bethsaida beside the Sea of Galilee. I had no intention of marrying him. But I had no other place to turn.

I moved with a sleepwalker's step upon that road, never once giving a thought to the fact that I could have been attacked by brigands. I bathed in brooks and ate berries from the more fertile slopes of the Jordan beyond the ford where the black rock pulpit stood empty against the sky.

At a small village I exchanged my few denarii for the robes of a Jewish peasant woman. The only tokens I saved from my former existence were the veils Marcus had given me. These I bound about my waist and arms beneath the Jewish clothing. In spite of the lewd way in which the bits of silk had been used, I couldn't bear to part with them. The merchant in the little shop where I bought the clothes gaped in astonishment when I presented him with my dusty finery after the change of costume.

He hadn't noticed the Roman cut of my clothes when I entered because I had kept my cloak about me. He was surprised to see I was probably not a Jew by birth. Clearly my dark hair and the few days I had spent in the sun made it possible for me to pass as one.

I left and once more turned my steps northward through the valley of the Jordan.

At times I prayed for a band of Sicarii to attack and slay me. Other times I felt a foolish confidence. It told me that somewhere I could find relief from my torment. Stumbling on, I hoped it was so.

I soon tasted for myself the authority of Rome which my mother was so eager to enforce. Between Hippos, a city of the Decapolis, and Bethsaida, a half-dozen military chariots came thundering down from the north. Their drivers lashed the horses shouting for people on the road to fall back. My legs ached from walking. I did not move fast enough. Racing abreast, the last two chariots thundered past. Their drivers laughed and shouted, having an impromptu race. Across the road a woman cried a warning in Hebrew. I wondered for whom the warning was meant—just as I saw that the chariot nearest me was swinging wide to avoid broken paving stones.

I was struck a glancing blow by the near wheel. It flung me head over heels among the brambles at the roadside. My head struck a rock. I gasped in pain. The sun blazed bright for an instant, then went out.

I awoke with a scent of cloves in my nostrils. A cloth redolent with wine was pressed to my lips.

"Praise be!" a woman's voice exclaimed. "She's not hurt after all."

"You're clucking over her as though she were your own daughter, Jesse," a man said.

A younger voice broke in, laughing.

"But, Father, Mother's always wanted a girl instead of a clumsy son."

"Hush, both of you," the woman said. "Joel, you good-for-nothing, fetch me the other wine jar from the summer room upstairs. Make a pallet ready so we can move her."

Opening my eyes, more than a little frightened, I said haltingly. "Who are you?"

The woman named Jesse, a wrinkled Jewess with a kind face, blinked in surprise.

"The child speaks Greek! She must come from a fine family."

"Is this a Greek household?" I asked.

The woman Jesse shook her head.

"This is the house of Micah ben Levi, half a day's journey from Bethsaida. We speak the tongue because of my husband." She indicated Micah standing beside her, a short, stout man with a bulb nose, small, dark eyes, and a friendly smile. "He's a fisherman. He sells his catches in Magdala and Capernaum. He has to converse in Greek though I've a mind to forbid him to deal with those Romans after the brutal way their chariots knocked you down."

The boy Joel came down the stairs from the upper room.

"Here's your jar, Mother." He was a handsome lad of about twelve, with broad shoulders and powerful tanned arms like his father's. "Have you learned her name yet?"

"Mind your manners, Joel," Micah said, though he looked just as interested.

"My husband and son carried you here after you fell," Jesse explained. "We thought you were badly hurt, but the cut on your forehead turns out to be a small one. I've already put ointment on it. Are you from this district? I don't recognize the cut of the kolbur."

She indicated the hem of my linen undergarment. Folding her arms, she stood back to wait for me to introduce myself.

I wasn't at all certain about what I should say or whether it was safe to tell the truth.

"My name is Salome. I—come from the south. Perea."

"Are you of our faith? asked Micah. "I see no emblems—"

"What difference does it make whether she's of our faith?" Jesse chided. "Yahweh has blessed us with a chance to help someone in distress. Had we not taken that journey to Hippos to visit my sister—which you, Micah, said was a waste of time—doubtless this poor girl would have lain at the roadside for hours. You saw how many people passed her simply because it's obvious she's not from this part of the country. Notice her skin. How delicate it is. What color she has comes from the sun."

"I beg your pardon," I interrupted, "but I'm feeling better now. I'll leave your house now. I don't want to bother—"

"You'll do no such thing," Jesse said.

The boy Joel chuckled. "This is Mother's grand opportunity."

Jesse looked concerned. "Have you a family, Salome?"

I averted my eyes. "No."

"Where did you live in Perea?"

"The household at Machaerus. I—I'm a Phoenician by birth. My father was killed in a shipwreck near the sunken port of Tyre. My kinsmen sold me into slavery. I ran away from the service of the tetrarch Herod Antipas."

"That monster!" Jesse exclaimed. "May Yahweh strike him dead."

"The tetrarch was responsible for the murder of the famous Essene preacher named John," Micah said. "We heard about it only yesterday. He was beheaded—"

"I know," I said softly, my guilt heavy again. "I heard of it the day after I escaped."

Joel's eyes were round. "What will they do to you if you're caught? Kill you?"

"They'll do nothing," Jesse said, "because she's going to stay with us as long as she wishes. Come, Salome. Let's go to the summer room upstairs. It's cooler. We'll have our evening meal on the roof when the sun goes down."

Putting her arm about my shoulders, she helped me toward the stairs. I tried to pull away. Once more I was sinking into a morass of lies, deception.

"I really can't accept your hospitality. I must go—"

"Where? Back to the household of Antipas to be punished? Nonsense. I won't hear of it. Here we go now, up the stairs—"

The touch of her hand was so comforting that my resistance melted. I went with the family to

199

the upper room, a cool place smelling of straw and the tang of the Sea of Galilee. I lay down on the pallet and slept until the stars came out, the first untroubled sleep I had known in weeks.

Thus, quite by chance I became a part of the household of Micah ben Levi.

Their sun-hardened mud home was scarcely a stone's cast from the blue waters in which Micah fished. It was a lovely place. Their roof commanded a view of the distant white buildings of Bethsaida in the distance. Out on the lake, fishing boats with scarlet sails darted about from sunup to sunset. One of the craft—with white sails—belonged to Micah. He and Joel rose at dawn, returning every night with bulging nets; they were highly skilled in their trade.

I fell easily into the household routine. I helped Jesse prepare meals and worked at the family loom, even becoming skillful at weaving under her guidance. It was a calm, happy existence. Not once did Jesse press me about my life at Machaerus, nor about my claim that my father had been a ship captain of Phoenician blood.

But happy and content though I was in the days and weeks that passed, I couldn't help but feel the respite was only temporary. I was still guilty of the death of the Essene, and there was still an emptiness within me that yearned to be filled. Sadly I came to realize that whatever it was that I must find in life would not be found in this simple household.

For days I tried to work up nerve to tell Jesse I must leave. To go where, I did not know. Perhaps Bethsaida, to seek council from Philip. Perhaps Jerusalem, in the hope that I might find Marcus.

But somehow I was unable to summon the courage to speak the words of parting.

Then early one morning an oak-shouldered man with a long beard burst into the house just before sunrise.

"Micah! Jesse! The Nazarene is near Bethsaida. Come with me to hear him."

Descending the stairs, Micah ran to clap the brawny man on the shoulder.

"Greetings, cousin Simon. We've scarcely seen you these past months."

"The fishing's been too good, Micah. But I'm not fishing today. Come, get ready. It'll take us nearly the whole day to reach the spot as it is."

The big man cast a friendly eye at me.

"Ah—a guest in your house?"

"Her name is Salome," Jesse said. "That's all you need to know. Tell me, is Jesus indeed nearby?"

Simon of Bethsaida nodded.

"He's resting on the plateau between the brooks of David, south near Hippos. The Pharisees were making it hot for him in Capernaum, so we decided it would be wise to go into the country awhile. I've walked nearly all night just to fetch you. Joel, put some bread into your pouch and let's be off." The big fisherman cocked a bushy eyebrow at me. "Your visitor can come too, if she wishes."

"Is this man of whom you speak, the Nazarene, called Jesus?" I asked.

"You've heard of him?"

"Many times. They say he's a marvelous physician."

Simon shook his head.

"Far more than that, child. When Jesus heals, it is with the touch of the Almighty."

"I for one want to see what this rabbi looks like," Micah said. "My nets can wait. Salome, would you like to come?"

"Please, if I may," I exclaimed. I hoped against hope that I might learn some secret of serenity from the rabbi whose presence excited them so. If Jesus the Nazarene could guide my steps to a path that would lead to the resolution of my terrible guilt, I would listen to him avidly—or to anyone else, for that matter. "Jesse"—I could hardly contain my eagerness—"Jesse—let me help you prepare food for the journey—"

Chapter II

Loaves and Fishes

As Simon the fisherman had predicted, the trip overland was long and hard. The Nazarene had retreated well into the countryside to avoid the attacks of the Jewish religious leaders who were antagonized by his strange new doctrines. But long before we neared the lonely plateau where twin brooks ran down toward the Sea of Galilee, it was apparent that hundreds of people knew where he was. When we reached the plateau toward the end of the day and saw the multitude gathered, young Joel let out a gasp of astonishment.

"Mother, there are several thousand here if there is one."

An odd light shone in Jesse's eyes. "It makes me wonder whether the stories that this man is the Messiah are really false, as the Pharisees in the temple tell us. Surely so many wouldn't come to hear a charlatan."

Simon shook his head, his face craggy with shadow and brooding in the late afternoon sunlight.

"This man's no charlatan, Jesse. This man is the son of our God come to earth."

Staring up into his sunburned face, I felt a shiver chase down my spine. In Simon I saw a strength of a kind I had never known. Fascinated, I pressed forward into the restless crowd and soon lost contact with Micah and his family.

The sun dipped near the lake and turned it scarlet. I had managed to make my way to the front of the crowd. At the water's edge, surrounded by several men in peasant costume, was the rabbi himself. He was clad in spotless white linen robes. His russet beard caught the sunlight, contrasting with the sunburned mahogany color of his face.

"What a handsome, gentle-looking man!" I exclaimed half aloud.

An attractive Jewess wearing several costly, colored girdles turned to smile.

"Indeed he is. There are some who would make his doctrine into a milksop's faith, but the Nazarene is a powerful man. Look at his arms. See—he's touching that crippled child. Almost a woman's touch—yet he could break a tribune's spine if he chose to do it."

204

"Why is he putting his hands on the boy?"

"To heal him."

"But he isn't a trained physician, is he?"

"Trained by God," the Jewess smiled. "A touch of those hands healed me of the seizures with which I'd been afflicted since I was a child in Alexandria. Have you ever noticed the fishing boats on the lake? The ones with red sails? They're mine—my fleet. Yet I'd be dead today— I'd have no boats, nor any life at all—if the master hadn't touched me."

"He actually cured you? That seems hard to believe—"

A tart smile curved the woman's mouth.

"Ask some of the people in the crowd, young woman. Ask them what kind of life Mary of Magdala lived before Jesus healed her. Then ask what sort of life she lives today. If that's not proof even the blindest Pharisee can accept, then life itself is a monstrous lie. Which I once believed— before I met him."

She turned an affectionate gaze toward the man on the shore. The crippled youth was up and running about now. I watched as he rushed into the arms of his weeping mother.

"See?" the rich woman said. "The limp is gone. How much more proof do you need?"

I turned my gaze back to the Nazarene. In his face and bearing, I saw the same tranquility I had glimpsed in John the Baptist, only intensified I felt it almost reach out and touch me like a physical force.

There were more wonders within the hour. Since the day's main meal for the thousands assembled came in the evening, the crowd grew

205

restive as the light waned. The followers of the Nazarene saw this, for they were examining in consternation their meager supply of food. It included a few loaves of bread and two fishes.

In the midst of their head-shaking, the Nazarene raised his hand, as though to indicate that they should compose themselves. For my own part, I was already counting on going hungry. I turned away, hoping to locate Micah and Jesse again.

Only a few minutes later, a voice cried, "There are loaves and fishes in plenty! See—loaves and fishes by the hundreds!"

Astonished, I watched the thousands press forward, hands outstretched, as great baskets of bread and fish were passed among them. I managed to snatch a bit of bread for myself. It was real enough. Where the food had come from I could not say. But everywhere there was talk of a miracle.

I spied Simon the fisherman distributing bread and hurried to his side.

"Simon, would your friend the Nazarene speak to me a moment? It's very important."

Simon shook his head. "There are so many who seek—"

He stopped, looking chagrined.

"Of course he'll speak with you. I've never yet seen him turn anyone away. Here, take my hand so we can navigate through this crowd."

Handing his basket to another, Simon led me down to the shore of the lake. The Nazarene was momentarily alone, the crowd being occupied with the bounty of fish and bread. Simon approached and told Jesus who I was and where I came from. The Nazarene smiled, a warm, manly smile of greeting, and gestured me forward.

Simon walked away. The Nazarene clasped my hand and led me still further down the shore, almost to the water's edge. The light of the sinking sun etched his strong profile with red light. Again a smile broke the rugged planes of his tanned face.

"You're troubled, child." His voice was soft and gentle. "It's as plain as the markings on a slate in the temple school."

"Rabbi, I have no right to speak to you because—well, because I lied to Micah ben Levi in the first place. I'm not a slave girl. I'm a Roman citizen. I know nothing of your god—"

"But, that's not true. Haven't you touched my hand?"

"I—"

No words would come for a moment. I stared into his face. Bursting like a dam, it poured out.

"I'm guilty, Rabbi. I committed a very great sin."

"You need say no more."

"I must explain—"

"John the Baptist is dead. You can't raise him to life. He would have been executed even if you hadn't made the request."

"*You know?*"

He nodded.

"But how is that possible?"

"All things are possible with God, Salome."

"Even forgiveness for such a crime as mine?"

"No person is without sin, Salome. Only God— and His love—are perfect. To find forgiveness, you need only acknowledge your sin."

"I'd acknowledge it a thousand times over, if that would help."

"It will. But that's only part of it. Love must be born within you. Not love of self, but the love of God and all his creatures—the kind of love that passes all human understanding. Love those who have wronged you. When they wrong you more, love them the more for it. But above all, love God."

Gently, he put his hand on my shoulder. He raised his face to the red heavens and murmured:

"Thy will, Father, and not mine be done. I have accepted thy will, for thou has sent me to earth to redeem sin. Put her sin upon my shoulders. I will bear it, together with all the sins of the world."

"You're a blessed man," I whispered, "A holy man—"

He smiled again. "It is God who is blessed and holy, Salome. When we become like Him, his blessedness and holiness are ours. They can be yours too."

Glancing up the shore, he indicated a blind woman being led to him by one of his followers.

"I must talk to others now. Your guilt will vanish if you live by my precepts. Go now—you're healed, just as surely as though you once walked with a twisted leg."

"Thank you, Rabbi," I began, trying to express the gratitude I felt. But before I could do so, he turned his attention to the blind woman. I walked away.

I felt he had given me a precious gift, a gift of hope. Could it be that by following his advice I might one day truly find forgiveness for my role in John's death? He had assured me it was so, if

208

only I would surrender myself to God. What were the words he had used?

Thy will, and not mine, be done.

I rushed through the crowd to find Micah and Jesse. *Thy will, and not—*

Abruptly, I stopped and thrust a hand to my mouth to keep from crying out.

On the far side of the throng, wrapped in his cloak and standing alone beneath a gnarled tree, was Thoth the Alexandrine.

The sight of him sent terror coursing through me. I drew my own cloak over my head and tried to lose myself in the crowd.

Why had Thoth journeyed this far north? There were only two explanations; perhaps both were equally valid.

One, Herodias was continuing to search for me. Two, she had sent her agent to spy on the Nazarene even though he had taken refuge in territory rightfully ruled by Philip. Herodias would overlook no opportunity to appraise threats to her ambition, and there was no longer any doubt in my mind that the Nazarene represented a power far mightier than that she sought to seize.

I debated silently about what I must do in the light of this new development. If Herodias actually planned to bring me back to Machaerus by force, the house of Micah ben Levi was no place for me, I didn't want to place Micah and his loved ones in danger if Herodias sent troops. Also, it would be easy for Thoth to trace me to the household. Perhaps word was already abroad that a Phoenician girl named Salome was living with the family.

I risked another glance toward the gnarled tree. The eunuch was gone.

Had he seen me? I didn't think so. But I didn't intend to give him a second chance. I hurried to the highest point on the plateau and found a hiding place among rocks. I stayed there until it was dark enough so that the Alexandrine would have difficulty spying me in the crowd. By then I had reached my decision—go to seek Marcus in Jerusalem.

In the city I would be less noticeable than I was in the Galilean countryside. Perhaps this time I could persuade him to run away. Together we could start a new and happier life in some distant country.

Immediately a problem presented itself. Reaching Jerusalem through territory infested by the Sicarii would be difficult. Their raids had become more frequent in recent weeks. On the long trek north from Machaerus I had given little thought to this danger and at times would have welcomed death at their hands. Now, however, the Nazarene had given me a glimmer of hope. But a return of hope also brought the return of fear.

Suddenly I thought of a solution. Since it was now dark, I felt safe enough to venture out among the crowd. Nowhere did I see Thoth among the small campfires, but I had no difficulty locating Simon of Bethsaida. He was apparently the Nazarene's foremost disciple. When people could not penetrate the crush around the rabbi himself, they turned to the big-shouldered fisherman for explication of Jesus' teachings.

At last I managed to draw Simon aside and

210

ask, "Do you know a man named Aaron of the Caves?"

Simon's brow knotted. "And if I do?"

"I must speak to him, as soon as possible. Please, Simon—help me in this. I once cut Aaron free when he was a prisoner. Now I need his assistance. Perhaps he'll return the favor."

"Better you'd left him tied up," Simon growled. "Everything the Sicarii stand for is opposed to the teachings of the man I follow—they want to put Jesus on a throne, raise an army, and throw the Romans out by force. Brutes like Aaron don't understand that the kingdom of Jesus isn't a kingdom of war engines and imperial trappings."

"But he's as much a subject of your god as you are, Simon."

"I can't deny that. But he certainly needs a lot of education."

"Can you find him? So that I can go to him?"

"Dangerous business for a woman, traveling about in the kind of places Aaron frequents," was his reply. He scratched his beard. "But since you're favored so highly by my cousin's wife, I'll do what I can."

"Thank you."

Simon shook his head.

"Thank the Nazarene for teaching a thick-witted fisherman like me to give the benefit of the doubt to men I despise. Now you should be off hunting Jesse—she's been searching everywhere for you. When I find Aaron, I'll send word."

He waved goodbye and vanished into the dark. I set about hunting the family of Micah ben Levi as he had suggested. I was unhappy at the prospect of leaving people who had treated me

211

with such kindness. I had to protect them. I had no choice.

And the Nazarene had given me hope for a new life. That life was Marcus, and the future we might yet win for ourselves, if only the past did not somehow rise up again to destroy everything.

Chapter III

Sicarii

In the weeks that followed, I went about my duties in the household of Micah ben Levi gripped by an impatience I could not completely conceal.

The sunlit days seemed to blend into one another in a pattern of maddening tedium. As I worked the loom or prepared food at Jesse's side, I could scarcely keep my eyes off the dusty road leading north to Bethsaida. Then one morning I was roused from my pallet by a tug of Jesse's hand. The stars had paled.

"I'm sorry I overslept, Jesse. You should have wakened me."

She shook her head. A tear lay on her wrinkled cheek.

"It was best you rested while you could. A man is waiting at the outer gate. He's to take you wherever it is you've yearned to go these past weeks. He's a villainous-looking fellow. Oh Salome—" She held me to her breast. "I wish God had given me a daughter like you. Must you really be gone so soon?"

"Yes, Jesse."

"But why?"

"It's better you don't know the reason. There are people searching for me. If you know nothing about me or where I've gone, you can tell the truth if they ever stop here. That way no harm will come to you. I'd kill myself rather than hurt you or Micah or Joel."

Jesse sighed. "I knew from the start that you were no slave girl. The silken girdles you wear about your waist are proof. Those veils could only come from a rich family, and I don't think you stole them. You're not the kind to steal."

I said, "For the lie I told you, I'm sorry."

"Salome, is there no way I can persuade you to remain?"

"None. Though I can truthfully say I wish you had been my mother."

Jesse wiped her eyes and reached beneath her robe. She brought out a small pouch of kidskin decorated with beads.

"Here, then, take this small gift. I started making it when I realized you were going to leave. Take it with my blessing. It should hold those veils you prize so highly."

Overwhelmed, I said, "You've truly learned the

214

Nazarene's lesson. I only hope I learn it as well."

"The Almighty attend your footsteps, Salome."

She stood up, about to say more when suddenly a flood of tears overcame her. She ran from the chamber.

I didn't go after her. To have done so would have made the parting all the more sorrowful. Instead I hurried down the outer stair to the gate. A raffish-looking man with matted hair and a leather patch over one eye was waiting.

He didn't bother to introduce himself. He motioned for me to climb onto the back of his verminous donkey. When I had done so, he jerked its rope and we set off down the road. Sunlight flashed on the curved dagger half-concealed by a fold of his hairshirt.

Well before we reached Bethsaida we turned off the Roman highway into a region of desolate hills. Grumbling incessantly, my guide led the donkey along a narrow defile and around a huge boulder. On top of the rock, cross-legged, sat another rascally specimen obviously standing guard. We passed around three more large rocks and came into the midst of the Sicarii camp.

About two dozen men lounged about the camp all armed with the familiar curved daggers. Next to the remains of a fire lay a half-devoured carcass of a lamb.

My guide dropped the halter rope and vanished into the mouth of a cave. The Sicarii made jokes in Hebrew, no doubt at my expense as I sat there on the fleabitten donkey. Presently a man emerged from the cave. I felt a rush of relief.

Aaron didn't smile. "What brings the daughter of the Romans to this camp?"

"The need of your help, Aaron. I've run away from Machaerus."

"So I heard," he replied. "Were it not so, you wouldn't have gotten within hailing distance of this place. But when Simon the fisherman sent word that a girl who had once helped me wished to see me, I gathered it must be you. Don't look alarmed. I said nothing to Simon's emissary about your identity. You may climb down and share our food, if you wish."

"No, thank you. Just tell me whether you'll help me reach Jerusalem. I don't want to travel the roads alone. But I must get there as soon as possible."

"Why?" he asked sharply.

"Is there no trust in you even yet?"

He shrugged. "One can't be too careful. Ordinarily I'd say no to your request. My work is too important to risk my men on a foolish errand. On the other hand, you gave me back my life. I owe you a debt. And it so happens I plan to go to Jerusalem myself. I have some—shall we say missionary work?—to do among backsliders of our group in the city."

He fingered the dagger at his waist. "The tender doctrines of the Nazarene have seduced too many Jews. If he's allowed to have his way, we'll all truckle to Rome and beg to kiss the backside of that bastard, Tiberius. For my part, I want a free nation, or none at all."

Growls of assent echoed from the campfire.

"Your politics are of no importance to me, Aaron, so long as you're willing to help me. How soon do you plan to leave for Jerusalem?"

"Two days from now."

He eyed his companions, many of whom directed hostile glances at me. Scratching his beard, he thought a moment longer, then said:

"It might be wise if we left sooner. You're a good-looking woman and my men haven't seen a woman in a long—well, you understand."

"Thank you, Aaron."

"Thank yourself," he said with a mocking grin. "You've shamed me into generosity I ordinarily wouldn't display. Hiram, stir up the coals and warm the remainder of the lamb. Obadiah, fetch the wineskin. Are you sure you don't want some food? It's not so fine as that at Machaerus, but at least it's purchased with our own sweat, not the blood of slaves."

Famished after the journey into the hills, I finally accepted his offer. I rested most of the afternoon in the shade of a rock, guarded by a pair of shaggy Sicarii upon whom Aaron kept close watch. With these two as escort, Aaron and I left the camp at sundown.

We were soon on the road leading south to Jerusalem. Aaron was not as rough a man as he pretended. He talked long on the history of his people, especially the feats of the warlike Judas Macabaeus of long ago. The trip passed with surprising speed.

The road leading down into Jerusalem was thronged with travelers. The roof of the temple gleamed golden in the distance. Now, Aaron confided, we must be more careful. No Sicarii would molest him—as none had molested us on the road—but to be caught carrying one of the curved daggers would mean instant death.

The house to which he led me was a dark,

walled place on a narrow street near the great
Damascus gate. The house belonged to a Jewish
tailor named Sholem. Aaron introduced me to a
grimy street boy who would carry a message anywhere in the city. Then Aaron saluted me with a
mocking wave of his hand and vanished, bound
on his own devious errands.

I instructed the boy carefully, making him repeat the number of the legion several times as
well as the whole message. He left. Then I sat
down to wait.

My heart beat hard within my breast, my
imagination conjuring all sorts of terrible fan-
tasies. I gripped the beaded pouch Jesse had made,
losing track of time, and evidently falling asleep.
Suddenly I started. The boy was trying to rouse
me. It was nearly sunset.

"The Fifth Legion has returned, Lady," he reported. "The man you're looking for is waiting on
the Royal Porch of the Temple. He seemed very
surprised when he got your message. He turned
white as a she-goat."

"Take me to him by the fastest route."

In an agony of anticipation I followed the boy
through the teeming streets. At last we pushed
our way into the Court of the Gentiles. The court
seemed unusually noisy and crowded for so late
in the day. There were many Roman soldiers
present. Quite a few of them smelled of wine. I
paid them little heed, intent on finding Marcus.

I spied him leaning against one of the white
marble pillars of the Royal Porch. My heart
leaped. I slipped a coin given me by Aaron into
the street boy's hand and ran the rest of the way
alone.

Chapter IV

Eagles in the Temple

Before I could speak, Marcus said stiffly:

"Why didn't you stay away from Jerusalem, Salome? Why tear open old wounds?"

"Marcus—beloved—I had to come. Don't be angry with me. It's been a hard journey. Oh, Marcus—"

I flung myself, burying my head against his chest, dimly conscious of complaints from several Pharisees on the porch. Drawing away from Marcus, I realized the reason—I was still dressed in the manner of a Jewess. Marcus noticed this for the first time.

"Does your mother ask you to wear this costume when you pay a visit to those less fortunate?" His voice was bitter.

"You don't understand, Marcus. I've left Machaerus."

"For the bedchamber of Philip the Tetrarch?"

"Will you be silent and listen to my words?"

"No. Not if I can't have you." His eyes swept over the restless throng in the Court. "I'd sooner go back into the desert this minute and scourge my flesh like an anchorite. Why should I torment myself by listening to you?"

Desperate, I seized his arm and drew him back into the shadow of the pillar.

"Marcus—I have left my mother *forever*. I'm not married to the tetrarch. I came from a household near Bethsaida, scarcely a day's journey from Philip's court. I could have gone to him—carried out the marriage bargain—but I came here instead. Don't turn me away. Not when everything else has gone bad. It's only because of you that I can even go on living."

But his face remained hard. "Salome, is this some joke? Some trick your mother forced you to play on me? That eunuch swore you were to marry Philip—"

"Philip's a good man, Marcus, kind—gentle. A man who'd help me if I asked—he would help anyone, in fact, were they friendless and in need. But I love *you*."

"Thoth said—"

"What he said, he was ordered to say—by Herodias."

Marcus' eyes widened.

"It was a trick, then?"

"Of course. And it worked. Perfectly. It turned you against me."

"But what brought you back to Jerusalem?"

Drawing a deep breath, I sketched the details of the death of John the Essene, not sparing my role in it. I told him of the events which had followed—my stay in the house of Micah ben Levi, my encounter with the Nazarene, and my journey back to Jerusalem to find him. As I told the tale his face changed, hard lines softened. When I finished he threw his cloak around my shoulders and pulled me close.

"The gods forgive me for doubting you," he whispered. "The gods forgive me—"

No longer were we the subjects of unwelcome attention. Most of the Jews had left the Royal Porch and gone into the court which had grown exceedingly noisy. Alone in the soft shadows of the white marble pillar, Marcus and I were free to kiss and share the sweetness of our reunion. A shudder of joy went through me as his strong arms gripped my waist.

"Beloved," I said, "you don't know how I've longed for you."

"And I for you, Salome."

Silent again, we clung together tightly for a timeless moment. When Marcus drew away, there was a shadow of unhappiness on his face:

"Salome, there's no getting around the fact I'm still a slave."

"We'll flee the city together."

"Do you know the penalty if I'm caught? Death. I couldn't bear to lose you a second time. That would be too cruel a—what's that noise?"

221

He stepped to the edge of the porch. "Curse them for drunken fools!"

"What's wrong?"

"Look for yourself. Yonder by the gate—"

"I see some soldiers milling in the crowd, that's all."

"But do you see what they're carrying? We have a loutish element in the Fifth. Pilate has given strict instructions that they're not to abuse the Jews, but the fools have been too long in the desert. Some of them have been drinking wine since dawn. They're spoiling for a fight."

"But what are they carrying?" I was unable to see more than a flash of metal in the dim red sunlight falling over the ramparts of Fortress Antonia. "Some sort of standard?"

"The eagles. Pilate has ordered that the eagles are never to be brought into the Temple. To the Jews, they're graven images. Once Pilate himself tried to bring them in and he nearly lost his life in a riot. Unless the tribunes can get that group outside, there'll be another one. Just listen to the crowd—"

The mob in the Court of the Gentiles had indeed grown angry. From every direction more Jews were rushing to the scene. Hundreds of them milled around the small band of Roman soldiers who had just entered the court. Suddenly I caught sight of a familiar face—Aaron of the Caves, whispering with one of his henchmen.

One of the Romans raised the eagle aloft. The crowd roared in anger.

For a moment the symbol of Imperial Rome burned scarlet against the sky. The screaming mob surged forward. The eagle standard fell. A second group of soldiers pushed in behind the first, yelling and brandishing still another eagle.

I saw Aaron slip through the crowd. A dagger flashed. The soldier carrying the second standard screamed. Blood spurted from his throat. He fell. The Jews stormed forward to trample him.

The Romans pulled their swords. They had seen their standard cast down, an unforgivable sin. The Jews had seen their Temple profaned, equally unforgivable. In another instant the scene erupted into a full-blown riot.

More armed legionnaires rushed down the staircase from the Antonia. They attacked the howling mob from the rear. The Jews turned upon them, bare-handed. Marcus' arm tightened on my shoulder.

I saw Aaron dart back to the fringe of the crowd, his dagger flying beneath the shield of a tribune to plunge into the man's belly. The tribune sprawled dead at his feet. Aaron leaped back, grinning triumphantly.

The Romans from Antonia pressed forward hacking ruthlessly with their swords. In turn, the Jews killed soldiers by sheer weight of numbers, falling on them like wolves and tearing them to pieces.

Another tribune crept up behind Aaron, sword raised. Aaron whirled. He dodged the first stab of the sword, but not the second. It plunged deep into his side.

Reeling back, Aaron almost fell. But he managed to stay upright and start for the street gate in a wobbling run. I saw two Sicarii break from the throng to help him. In another moment all three were lost from sight.

Instantly I knew what must be done. I seized Marcus' arm.

"Did you see that man just struck by the tribune?"

Marcus nodded. "One of the Jewish zealots. He deserves what he got."

"He's the man who helped me reach Jerusalem —Aaron of the Caves."

Marcus gaped. "That murderer?"

"Marcus, he was badly hurt. You're a doctor. We must go to him. Help him."

"Help a Jewish brigand?"

"He was kind to me. He deserves help just as much as any of your soldiers."

"But he's an *enemy!* My duty is to the legion."

Suddenly I knew that if I failed now, I would fail in everything.

"Marcus, listen to me. Remember the Nazarene I spoke of? He told me we must help those who hate and scorn us. Only then can we be free of the evil we've done."

"I've done no evil as far as the Jews are concerned—" Marcus began.

"But I have! Please help me. I know where Aaron will go—"

Unhappily he surveyed the struggling mob. The fighting had grown less violent as reinforcements poured down from the Antonia. Finally he gave a reluctant shake of his head.

"I don't understand you, Salome. Not even on the grounds that a physician's duty transcends his duty to an organization like the legion. But if it's what you want—lead the way."

I clasped his hand in mine and we made our way around the edge of the crowd to the street

224

below the Temple. Marcus had drawn his cloak over his uniform to hide it, and once we had escaped the confusion in the Temple area, we found the going easier.

We arrived at the house of Sholem the tailor in lowering darkness. For many moments no one answered my knock. Then at last Sholem himself appeared, his face wrinkled with suspicion.

"Let me in, Sholem," I said. "I've brought a doctor for Aaron."

"The Sicarii are not here," Sholem said. "They have gone."

"Don't lie, old man. I know Aaron's here. He couldn't go far with the kind of wound he took in the Temple. Let us in."

Sholem wrung his hands, but he admitted us and locked the gate. I led Marcus toward a room where a lamp glowed, the tailor's workroom just off the court. One of Aaron's companions leaped up as we entered. His eyes narrowed at the sight of Marcus' armor. He thrust a dagger against my throat.

"You'll die for bringing a Roman to this house, girl."

"This man is a physician. Let him look at Aaron. Where is he?"

Bewildered, the zealot gestured.

"Over there, behind the hanging."

Scowling, Marcus flung his cloak aside and jerked the woven curtain back.

Aaron lay sprawled on a stone couch inside an alcove, his skin pale in the gleam of the oil lamp. His tunic was covered with blood.

Marcus knelt down. I marveled at the way his

hostility left him the moment he was in the presence of an injured man.

Marcus called for water and cloths as he began ripping away Aaron's garments. The man who had stopped us at the door stared incredulously until I jogged his elbow.

"Send your companion to fetch water, or go yourself!"

"Jezreth is not here," the man said. "He fell behind. The Romans took him." He stumbled out.

Aaron groaned, throwing his forearm across his eyes. Marcus stood up, shaking his head.

"There's little I can do for him, Salome. The wound is too deep."

The Sicarii stumbled into the room with a basin and strips of wool. These last Marcus began to bind around the wound to slow the leak of blood. From Aaron's cries, it was clear that he was not many moments from death.

Marcus' face had gone white with concern. This was not a dying Jew but a dying man, and Marcus stood helpless and angry before the spectacle of death's victory.

Opening the little case he carried on his belt he produced a bit of root which he tried to thrust between Aaron's lips. Instantly the other Sicarii leaped forward, dagger drawn.

"What are you feeding him?"

"Mandrake. If he chews it, it may ease his dying."

"*Dying—?*"

"That's what I said."

With a curse of despair the Sicarii flung his dagger away and sat down in the corner, burying his face in his hands.

Marcus crouched down beside the writhing man. He gripped Aaron's jaw between his hands, forcing him to chew the root. Presently Aaron's thrashing grew less violent. His hand flopped over the edge of the couch. He turned his head slightly. His eyes opened.

"It hurts less now," he gasped. "Thank Yahweh for that much. Benjamin?" He touched Marcus' face.

"My name is Marcus Catullus. I'm a doctor from the Antonia."

"A doctor from——?"

Aaron struggled up in spite of Marcus' efforts to restrain him. His eyes went wide, lucid for an instant. He took in Marcus' uniform and trappings, then fell back.

"I never thought—a Roman—but thank you."

Aaron's head rolled to the side. His eyes widened again, full of wonder as he stared at the enemy who had come to his aid. "Thank you."

"Try not to talk," Marcus wiped Aaron's forehead with wool dipped in water. "If the pain becomes too severe, I've a little more of the root left."

Suddenly Aaron screamed:

"Hold my hand. Take my hand——"

Aaron reached out blindly. Marcus took his hand. Aaron's fingers closed around it, childlike. Marcus turned to look at me, his eyes questioning. His voice became a mumble.

"It's dark. God preserve me—it's getting dark. I'm afraid. I don't like the dark. Hold my hand so I won't lose my way——"

Aaron fell back. His mouth dropped open. Slowly, Marcus let go of the pale hand.

When he turned from the alcove after drawing the hanging back into place, Marcus' face was bewildered. He shook his head, as though he could not quite comprehend why an enemy had wanted to hold his hand in the moment before death. But I understood. I had seen the Nazarene's miracle of love come to pass just as surely then as if Marcus had raised Aaron from the dead.

Hammering began at the street gate. Instantly the other Sicarii jumped up.

"Jezreth! The Romans must have caught him and loosened his tongue. Quick! Where's the old man? Sholem? Sholem—answer!"

From the front of the house came the racket of splintering timbers and the shouts of Roman soldiers running through the court. Marcus spied another doorway in the room. We started for it. The first of the legionnaires burst in.

"One of them's even dressed like a Roman! Antipater, the rest of you—kill all three of them!"

Marcus stepped forward. "Wait. I belong to the—"

"You belong in a grave, traitor!" shrieked one of the soldiers swinging a whip in his right hand.

Too late Marcus tried to dodge. The iron barbs at the end of the thongs raked his face open. Marcus screamed and staggered against a wall as the soldiers crowded in upon him.

The stab of a sword would have ended his life had not the other Sicarii lunged into the path of the blade. The Sicarii took the thrust meant for Marcus. The soldiers darted back to avoid the gouting blood. I ran to the alcove for the oil lamp. I dashed its contents over the Romans, then threw the lamp itself.

A soldier's cloak burst into flames. He shrieked. The Romans began stumbling over one another. I took Marcus' hand and led him to the second doorway. A moment later we found ourselves in a fetid alley behind Sholem's house. Clutching his face, Marcus could barely walk.

"Marcus! We must keep going or we'll never get away!"

A moan of pain, a moan that broke my heart, was the only sign that he understood. We hurried along the dark alley while I pulled his cloak over his head.

We huddled down behind a gate a few houses from Sholem's. A moment later the soldiers ran past crying the alarm. When they had gone, I helped Marcus to his feet.

Luckily the soldiers had not yet barred the Damascus gate. We stumbled through, Marcus shuddering against my shoulder.

We walked until Jerusalem lay far behind. Only the empty night lay ahead.

Chapter V

Oasis of Despair

In the first perilous hours after we slipped through the gate at Jerusalem, I exulted in our freedom. At dawn I begged a flask of wine and a joint of meat near the village of Jaba. The wine helped Marcus, relieving the pain that had tormented him as he stumbled at my side all night long, one of the silken veils clutched to his mangled face.

As the sun rose he lay panting against a rock. I stripped away the veil—and stifled a gasp of horror.

"Is it that bad?" he asked. "Better to leave me

here then. I don't want you burdened the rest of your days with a monster—"

"Nonsense. Stop feeling sorry for yourself. We're together, and that's all that matters. Drink some more wine. Then tell me which of the ointments in your kit I can use to make a poultice. The bleeding's stopped at last. I'll go to the stream beyond these rocks, fetch water and clean you up. Then we'll apply the medicine and rest here all day. We can travel at night."

"Travel where?"

"Wherever the legions won't follow."

"That can only be eastward. Into the desert."

"Then eastward it is."

I looked into his ruined face and tried to show him that I would love him no matter what happened. It wasn't just the look of him I loved, but the man beneath. He reached up to touch the ruin of his cheek. I caught his wrist.

"Don't do that, Marcus. I don't care about your face. I care about you."

"How can we live? We'll starve out here or be killed by wild animals."

"Let me worry about that until your face heals. After that I know you'll be strong enough to gather food to feed us both, and take care of any marauders in the bargain. It'll be an ordeal for awhile. But if we're together, we can get through it."

Marcus studied me skeptically.

"I wish I had the courage you seem to have."

"It's not mine, Marcus. I got it from a very wise man."

"The rabbi you met at Bethsaida?"

"Yes."

"Do you suppose he would give me enough strength that I could look on my own face again?" Marcus sneered.

I tried to ignore the pain in his voice and stretched out my hand. "I have the strength for both of us. His strength is born in love. Come, walk with me to the stream. Look at your face once and forget about it."

He kept his hand at his side.

"Marcus?"

"No. I can't look at my face. Not yet—or I'll never take another step along the road you want us to travel."

His pain was so great, his pride so wounded, that I thought it best not to pursue the matter. Instead I made him as comfortable as I could in a patch of shade. I pulled aside the first bloodied veil and went to dampen the second in the nearby stream.

When I returned, he greeted me with an empty smile. I decided then and there that I would need the strength of two if we were to bear the next few weeks.

Our destination was unknown. Once we were out of the jurisdiction of Rome and Marcus had begun to mend, there would be ample time to look for a village where we could live unnoticed. How we would live—what trade Marcus would follow—those questions had to be put aside for the moment. Only escape mattered—escape and bringing him back to life.

Traveling by night, we crossed the Jordan and pushed eastward.

One by one the silken veils dropped behind, daubed with blood and sticky with the white oint-

ment Marcus had instructed me to apply. We had
no trouble begging food, there being only a few
villages in which I could not find some elder who
spoke Greek. We did not really grow hungry until
the face of the land began to change from fertile
to arid. The villages were farther apart now, the
land sandy; the sun grew hotter. Marcus' face,
which had shown signs of healing, became irritated by the blowing sand in spite of the veils I
kept bound around it. It began to itch and weep.
Some times he grew almost delirious with pain.
But there were no roots in his kit to ease the
hurt. He had given them all to Aaron of the
Caves.

The villages disappeared altogether. We had
wandered into a trackless desert. Instead of
growing better, Marcus grew worse. Caked with
dirt from head to foot, glassy-eyed and stubble-
cheeked, he staggered at my side like some pitiful
wreck from the dungeons of Machaerus. My own
strength ebbed. A supply of berries and wine we
had hoarded was fast dwindling.

The dunes stretched on endlessly. The sun
burned molten. Soon, I kept telling myself, soon
we'll find sanctuary, even though it be in the
tents of the Bedouins. These were hooded desert
men we had seen riding on the skyline once or
twice.

They are wise, I thought. Skilled in medicine.
Many of their teachings have come to Rome.
They will help us—

Then the desert spirits lifted the sand against
us.

For two days and nights we wandered in a
shrieking oblivion of wind-whipped sand. Marcus

233

cried aloud, no longer in possession of his wits. Time and again I helped him to his feet, only to have him fall again. Finally we sank down, unable to continue.

I pulled the tatters of his cloak over us, the taste of sand in my mouth, thick and gritty on my eyelids. I held his wasted, shuddering body close to mine and prayed to a nameless god to deliver us.

At last the swollen ball of the sun appeared behind the dancing curtain of sand. In the distance I saw spiky palms standing black against the dun-colored sand. I cried out aloud in joy. For a moment I thought my eyes had deceived me. But they hadn't. It was an oasis, with a dry depression in the center to indicate where a pool of water had once sprung. We reached the shelter of one of the palms as the storm began to lessen.

I dropped to my knees, digging my hands deep into the natural cup, and drew them forth moist and covered with dark, damp sand.

"Marcus, we're saved! There's water below. It will soon seep to the surface and—*Marcus!*"

He had fallen on his back, mouth open. The last of the silk, the scarlet one, flapped in the hot wind, revealing the festering wreckage of his cheek. Frightened, I put my ear to his chest. He was still breathing, but I could not rouse him.

The storm blew out. The sky cleared. I lay across Marcus' body, sobbing over the futile journey we had taken.

We had reached the end—I had no illusions about that now. We would probably die in this very spot. All that remained for me to do was to make the passing of the man I loved as bearable as possible.

I lifted the last veil from his face. He moaned as bits of flesh tore away and the bleeding began again. Dampening the veil in the seepage beginning to fill the depression, I moistened his wounds and covered them with the wet silk. From the kidskin purse at my girdle—the one Jesse had given to me—I took a few berries, our last food, and forced them one by one through Marcus' lips.

As the sun climbed, the heat became unbearable. I moved every few moments, trying to keep Marcus in the shadow of my body. I was not aware of night coming on because I had fallen over into the sand, sick with weakness myself.

In the night I dreamed strange dreams. The face of the Nazarene shone from a vast black cloud. When I woke at dawn, with the stars glimmering and the sun already smoldering on the horizon, I composed myself, because I knew it was only a matter of one or two days at most before we died. At least it would be together.

Alternately I slept and wakened. The waking was more like a dream than anything else. Objects blurred in the scalding sunlight. Even the outline of Marcus' head in my lap began to shimmer and waver.

As the sun hung nearly overhead I thought I saw a line of horsemen passing far to the east. Several of them seemed to ride toward the oasis, then doubled back. The heat overcame me again. When I roused at nightfall, they were gone. I realized they must have been illusions.

The setting of the sun brought little relief. I was too numb to move the cloak covering us.

Marcus breathed thinly. I found myself praying death would be quick and merciful.

But it was not to happen that night. At the next dawn I saw a seething cloud of dust on the western skyline. It rolled steadily closer.

Another storm? Or only another mirage?

Any moment I expected the cloud to vanish. When it didn't, I realized it was far too localized to be a sandstorm. Disbelieving, I stared at the vehicle that rolled in the forefront of the teeming cloud.

It was a light Roman chariot of war, driven by a Roman soldier.

"Marcus!" I cried, shaking him. "Marcus, wake up! There are people coming!"

He only moaned.

I turned to see a dozen more chariots break from the cloud followed by a line of weary foot soldiers.

In a moment my joy changed to fear. Marcus still wore the vestiges of his legion costume—his tunic and the tattered leather flaps of his girdle. His cloak lay beside him.

Behind the foot troops rolled baggage wagons. It was not a single patrol that had ventured this far eastward, but a small army. No matter what the danger, I must appeal to the soldiers for aid—only that way could I save Marcus' life.

Hastily I dug a pit in the sand, buried cloak, girdle and tunic out of sight. Left only in his clout and covered by the veil I had taken from his face, he presented a sorry sight.

The cumbersome wagons, bogged nearly to their axles in the sand, had come to a halt. An eagle standard blazed in the sunlight. Pavilions were being erected by some of the foot soldiers. A line of the foot troops marched steadily toward the oasis. The war chariots had swung south around the oasis and were continuing east, as though to survey the terrain ahead. I shaded my eyes to gain a better look at a stocky figure in the leading chariot. My stomach knotted in terror.

At the head of his troops, cloak flying as he stood with one arm about his charioteer's waist, rode Herod Antipas.

Chapter VI

Reunion

His beard had grown long and unkempt, and had turned nearly white. He waved to his charioteers, urging them to greater speed. Something about his manner, perhaps the defiant stance or his wild shouts, confirmed that the army was being led by a madman. For only a madman would bring baggage wagons and chariots and foot troops burdened with armor into a desert where such equipment could only be an encumbrance.

A hush fell over the foot troops who had stopped near the oasis. They had seen me. But they hung back while their tribune hauled out his sword and called to his men.

"She's no Nabatean wench, that I can tell. Amvis, Justa—forward with me, in case it's a trick."

Three swords winked in the sun as the trio advanced. They started visibly when they saw Marcus. The youngest soldier barely kept from retching at the sight of his face.

"This man needs help," I said. "Where is your physician?"

"Dead," the tribune snapped. "A maddened horse kicked him to death two nights ago. I'm the one to ask the questions. Who are you? You speak Greek like an educated woman—"

"Please give him assistance—"

"She might be a spy, sent out by the enemy," said one of the soldiers.

"Where do you come from?" the tribune demanded.

"My husband and I came here by way of the village of Jiza."

"You're not Jews—" he began suspiciously.

"In the name of the gods, stop talking, give him some water! He's almost dead."

"Well—" The tribune scowled. "I suppose a drink won't do any harm. Amvis, pour a little down his throat."

Pale, the youngest soldier unhitched a skin pouch at his waist and knelt beside Marcus. The tribune caught my wrist.

"I want answers, woman. Who are you and what brings you here?"

"We're only pilgrims. We lost our way."

"They certainly can't have any weapons hidden in this godforsaken place," said another soldier.

"Unless she's carrying King Aretas and his entire army under that one ragged garment."

"Aretas!" I exclaimed. "Are these his lands?"

"Aye," the tribune replied. "And we're too far over his borders to suit me. But then I only take orders from our illustrious leader. I won't take the responsibility for aiding strangers though. Antipas might have me whipped, considering the way his mind works—or fails to work—lately. Bringing an army into this desert—pfaugh!" He spat in the sand. "A fool's errand. We'll all die before he recognizes his folly."

"At least summon a soldier with your medical supplies."

"Go plead your case yourself, woman."

"But Antipas has ridden out with the chariots," said the young soldier. He had just poured water over Marcus' lips; with no apparent effect.

"Then she can go grovel before that madwoman he drags with him," the tribune exclaimed, starting away.

"Is the wife of Antipas with the army?"

"His whore, you mean?" said the tribune, his temper growing short. Sweat poured down his cheeks from under his helmet. "She goes everywhere with him. She's the reason we're out here in the first place. King Aretas repaid the insult of having his daughter Nefer cast out. Antipas isn't content to have the Nebateans attack us on our own ground where we have a chance—oh, no. He listens to that shrew Herodias and drags good men into this hell to put on a show of strength."

"Surely we could make this man comfortable before we go back to raise camp," said the

240

younger soldier, still kneeling beside Marcus. "Surely Antipas wouldn't whip us for that."

"Will you take the lash if he decides these people are dangerous? No, I'll be the one who suffers. Leave the water. I'm making an official report before I lift another finger. Get a move on, both of you. The sun will broil us all if we don't raise the shelters."

So saying, he stalked away from the oasis.

He was quickly followed by the other two. I could understand his reluctance to bring down the wrath of my mother and Antipas. It would a doubly terrible wrath in such a fearsome place— but it was a wrath I must face. I was willing. I would bear any humiliation—any pain or punishment—if only my mother would save Marcus' life.

I turned my steps westward toward the pavilions being erected there. This was the test of the Nazarene's teaching—to face with compassion my most dreaded enemy.

For the site of their camp, the foot troops had chosen a steep dune which afforded a little shade. The dune cut off my view of the camp as I left the oasis. I passed unobserved by those on the other side of the hill. I heard them complaining about the tyranny and foolhardiness of their leader.

From the colors of the central pavilion, I knew I would find my mother inside. Two soldiers raised spears as I approached. One of them thrust the point against my breast.

"Who's this?" he said to his companion. "Some Nabatean bitch?"

"A Roman citizen, and mind your filthy tongue."

Both men burst out laughing. Enraged, I ducked under the point of the spear and slapped the first man's face.

"Tell Herodias that her daughter Salome waits upon her."

Their mouths dropped open.

"Her *daughter?*"

In a swirl of color the pavilion hangings were swept aside. There stood my mother, resplendent in a yellow robe and green girdle.

Except for a gleam of perspiration on her brow, she might have been a courtesan facing Tiberius at Capri, so calm was her face. But it was a frightening calm; I detected paleness beneath her kohl-blackened eyes, and a glitter in the eyes themselves that told of strange twistings in her mind since I had seen her last. One of the soldiers mumbled:

"This dirty creature professes to be your daughter, Lady. Shall I tie her to one of the wagons?"

A curious, almost dreamy smile played on my mother's lips. She raised a hand in a courtly gesture, pearl and sapphire rings gleaming.

"She is my daughter. Let her pass."

Thunderstruck, the soldiers stood aside. I did not want to go into the dark pavilion—the gleam in my mother's eyes was too strange and fearful.

Then I thought of the serene expression on the Nazarene that night beside the Sea of Galilee. I found the strength to master my fear, and went in without looking back.

My mother followed. Standing still, I waited

for her to speak. Instead, she surveyed me in silence a moment more.

"What words can possibly serve to describe this miracle, Salome?"

"I can't say whether finding you is a miracle or not, Herodias. That will depend on what happens now."

"Salome, you angered me terribly."

"Is that the mood in which you receive me— anger?"

"Salome, Salome, my child—"

Through the wall of coldness she had erected about herself broke a faint gleam of humanity. She lifted her arms wide, then her eyes changed. Into them came a look as close to madness as any I had ever seen.

"To find you this way—lost in this ugly land! How far you must have come! Your feet are bruised—they must be cleansed. We must have a joyful reunion."

Fighting back nausea and weakness which threatened me in the stifling air of the pavilion, I shook my head. "First you must help me, Herodias."

"Speak the word *Mother*, Salome, not my name.

I wanted to retort that she had never deserved nor earned the name *Mother*. Some power greater than myself held me back. I said:

"Help me, Mother. Marcus lies at the oasis, near to death."

Her eyes grew wide.

"Marcus? He came with you here?"

"From Jerusalem. It's a long, painful story, and there's no time to tell it now. He's almost beyond help." My voice rose uncontrollably. "You owe me this much, Mother—payment for the night the Essene died at Machaerus. I don't ask it for my sake. Only for Marcus' life. Then you can do what you will with mine."

A flicker of contempt darkened her gaze.

"I gave you up for dead, Salome. I never again expected to have a daughter sit at my side." She put her arms about me. I could not tell whether her words sprang from a long-dead emotion I had somehow roused, or whether her tongue only shaped her speech to fit still one more plan for advancing her husband's cause.

"I want you with me always. Don't run from me again. Promise you won't. Swear it."

I closed my eyes. Deep inside, I felt a great hurt.

"Is that your price, for helping Marcus?"

Softly: "Yes."

"All right. I'll pay it. Just help him."

She clapped her hands. Startled, I whirled about as a familiar figure emerged from the shadows.

Thoth.

His tunic was black with sweat. His bald skull shone with it, as he surveyed me from head to foot. Herodias lifted the hanging at the pavilion's entrance.

"Young Marcus Catullus lies hurt at the oasis. Go with Salome and bring him here."

Thoth bowed. "As you wish, Lady."

He cast an eye to the heavens. They had grown gray again during the time I talked with my mother.

"We must make haste, Mistress Salome. The sand will blow again soon."

Shivering uncomfortably in his presence, I followed him outside. He marched ahead, his great splayed feet raising dust that danced on the wind. Behind the dune that hid the oasis from view, I heard the foot troops noisily securing their shelters in the teeth of the rising storm. Northward, the chariots could be seen racing back toward the camp.

At the oasis Thoth knelt beside Marcus, made a cursory examination, then rose. He stood stock still in the wind.

"Pick him up, Alexandrine. There's no time to be lost."

"His life will keep a moment longer," was the reply.

"I order you to pick him up at once."

"Not until I keep a promise I once made myself."

"Promise? What promise?"

A smile twisted his lips. "That I would possess your body, Mistress. It no longer shines softly, but that makes no difference. For years you have fought me, secretly as well as openly, in the household of the woman I serve. In that household I rose to a position of pre-eminence. Only you stood against me. Yet I desired you. Is that not curious, little Mistress? Thoth the eunuch, desiring you?"

"Madman!"

"Our little game is almost played out, Mistress. Its conclusion shall give me a double pleasure. It will fulfill a wish first conceived one day when I spied on you bathing naked in the peristyle back

245

in Rome. You were only a small child, with budding breasts. At the same time I can repay you for making my path a difficult one."

"What black gods put this monstrous idea in your mind?"

A fat yellow hand plucked at the girdle of his tunic, loosening it. "One whose manhood is ruined by the knife has many strange thoughts."

"But how can you—" I shook with fright. "You, half a man—"

"There are ways, Mistress." His face shone out of the murk of the gathering storm. "Oh, yes, there are ways. I have waited long to try them."

He walked toward me. I looked about for some weapon, but there was none. We were cut off from the shelters of the legionnaires. Even the loudest scream wouldn't be heard above the wind.

His hands shot out, gripping my wrists. He pulled me toward his huge belly. The sweat-and-spice stink of his flesh filled my nostrils. I began to scream and struggle.

He was powerful. He drew me ever closer to the heaving obscenity of his body, leaning down toward me, his lips shining with spittle, parted and eager—

Suddenly he stiffened.

He took a halting step, then another. He stared at me in disbelief. His legs twisted beneath him, and he fell. Buried in folds of fat at the nape of his neck was a feathered arrow.

His tunic flapped in the wind. Another arrow bit solidly into the trunk of the palm under which Marcus was lying.

Out of the storm in the east rumbled the war chariots of King Aretas of the Nabateans.

Chapter VII

Battle

Thoth's head was twisted on his neck. His open mouth slowly filling with sand. Already Marcus was half-covered. The sudden storm had nearly obscured the sun.

From the Roman camp came confused shouting, the rumble of wheels, and the neighing of horses as the soldiers prepared to meet the attack of the Nabateans, an attack that had undoubtedly been timed to coincide with the storm.

Chariots bearing the warriors of King Aretas streaked past me on either side. From the car of the nearest, one of the desert men let forth a hideous shriek and flung a spear at my head. I threw myself out of the way.

The tip grazed my face. I dropped to the ground and covered my head as flying hoofs thudded past and sand rained down on me. I missed being crushed by the wheels by the barest margin.

The sting of the wound on my face roused me, and gave me strength to crawl to Marcus. I wiped sand from his face and shoulders. His breathing was so faint as to be nearly inaudible. I cradled his ravaged head against my breasts.

He let out a groan. I found myself crying—and wishing him dead. A swift, merciful passing would be better than whatever lay in store for us after this fearful battle.

The small detachment of Roman foot soldiers was no match for the Nabatean chariots. The foot troops retreated almost at once. Three more chariots went thundering through the oasis. One driver held a lighted torch that streamed in the wind. Guiding his horses with one hand, he flung the torch with the other. High in a palm it ignited the dry fronds and set them blazing.

Shrill orders flew back and forth between the attacking chariots. The Nabatean lines began to reform just west of the oasis, the desert men using the burning tree as a signal beacon in the murk.

That the battle had turned almost at once in favor of the forces of King Aretas was apparent from the screams from the Roman lines and the exultant cries of the desert warriors. Then, without warning, the Nabatean chariot drivers whipped their animals fiercely to bring them into line. The armed men riding behind each driver leaped down and rushed forward, crude spears and curved swords ready.

I soon saw the reason for the new formation. A dozen Roman chariots—nearly the entire force—came careening over a dune straight for the Nabatean lines.

The Romans were racing toward almost certain destruction. The Nabatean chariots outnumbered them three or four to one. Still they came on, only two men to a chariot, the driver with the reins lashed around his waist, both men holding a spear in one hand and a sword in the other.

The Nabateans on foot lunged foward at the last instant and struck upward with their blades. The Roman chariot teams met a wall of curved steel. Horses dropped, their bowels hanging from ripped bellies, while foam spilled from their teeth and flew from their manes. A Nabatean took a Roman spear through the chest. A moment later the Roman was cut open from throat to navel by a desert man who had climbed over the side of the stalled chariot.

Only four Roman vehicles broke through in that dreadful charge. They converged in a dash to the oasis. I tried to crawl back into the scant protection of the palm as I saw that two of the chariots would collide. One driver cried a warning, too late. The chariots locked wheels and broke apart in a hideous rending of wood and metal.

One charioteer was trampled beneath the hooves of his frantic team. The other driver and the two soldiers were quickly dispatched by the Nabatean swordsmen. The pair of chariots which got through disappeared into the storm, circling back in a desperate attempt to rejoin the Roman host. Far out in the murk I heard screams to signal their failure. In moments, complete disaster had overtaken Herod Antipas.

Wild with triumph, the hooded desert men wheeled their chariots back through the oasis. Torch bearers set fire to the wreckage of the Roman vehicles. Flame licked out toward the palms. The oasis was illuminated by a fierce fire that would soon sweep everything before it.

A hand caught my hair. I was jerked to my feet. One of the hooded men turned me around, holding me like a toy. His pointed white teeth shone with savage mirth. He yelled to his comrades, who quickly surrounded me.

One Nabatean reached beneath my gown to my breast. The man holding me flung me over his shoulder and leaped into a chariot already gathering speed for a retreat from the burning oasis.

Wind howled in my ears, sand blinded me, fire licked at me with orange tongues as the chariot went plunging through a blazing barrier of trees. I screamed:

"Marcus—"

The chariots thundered out of the oasis. They tilted sickeningly as the teams dragged them over the crest of the dune from which they had attacked. Hanging on my captor's shoulder, too weak to struggle, I had a last view of the pillar of fire in the storm. If I could have found strength to cry, I would have done so.

The chariots dipped down the far side of the dune. If these men must kill me, I thought, let it be quick. I have borne enough. But then I remembered certain words, and while I could not recall their origin or their precise meaning, they had a comforting sound. I repeated them to myself until, in some miraculous way, I drew strength from them:

"Thy will be done—not mine. Thy will be done—not mine."

The chariots stopped abruptly. I was handed from one Nabatean to another, and finally set on the ground. Here in the shelter of the high dune, the fury of the sandstorm was less severe. It was possible to see things in some detail. But what I saw set my teeth to chattering.

They ringed me like bearded wolves. Several had their burnooses thrown back. They nudged one another, speaking in a queer tongue I did not understand. But what they planned was all too clear.

Gathering my spent strength, I snatched at a dagger hanging in a sheath from the girdle of the man who had carried me on his shoulder. I tore the blade free, and was close to driving it into my own breast when another man seized upon my wrist. Viciously, he twisted the knife away. He threw it over his shoulder toward a silken pavilion. Then he tore the remnant of my gown from top to bottom.

I tried to hold the tatters together to conceal my nakedness. The warriors laughed. I gathered I was to be the prize of every one of them before I died.

My captor wiped his lips with his forearm. This produced another peal of mirth from the men. He flung me to the ground and stood over me, grinning.

I closed my eyes. *Thy will—*

A voice, strong and sharp, yet oddly pitched for a man of the desert, came to my ears then. Every lustful growl was suddenly silenced.

The new voice barked commands. A second, deeper voice seemed to repeat the phrases. I turned to look.

At first I didn't recognize the woman standing above me, for she wore a robe similar to those of the tribesmen. It was thrown open, however, and above her scarlet girdle her breasts were bare. Bangles clanged when she gestured for two of her soldiers to bring me to my feet.

"Nefer!"

"Am I cursed with visions in the hour of victory?" She spat in Greek. "Is this the daughter of Rome who confronts me?"

I drew a deep breath. "Yes, Nefer, I am Salome, daughter of Herodias."

"Then my eyes haven't tricked me."

Nefer whirled and spoke to her warriors. With words and gestures they gave what I took to be an account of my capture at the oasis. An older man behind her, a hook-nosed patriarch with flowing beard and embroidered robes, listened closely. I heard someone speak the name Aretas.

When Nefer had satisfied herself about my capture, the old man asked her several questions. She gestured angrily toward the camp of Antipas as she spoke.

Understanding dawned on the face of the desert king. His expression grew fierce. Nefer turned back to me. Her eyes were filled with hate.

"A kind heaven has delivered you to me. Antipas is only a man, weak, easily twisted in his thinking. But you—you are one of the harlots who drove me from his house. I shall find it much more satisfying to kill you."

Chapter VIII

Thy Will Be Done

I had strength to say only, "Do what you will
with me, Queen Nefer."

"Believe me, I shall. In privacy—where I may
enjoy it properly."

She clapped her hands. Her warriors pushed
me forward. I was conscious of an immense weariness as I walked in Nefer's pavilion. I only
hoped I could die with some scrap of dignity and
courage.

At the pavilion entrance, Nefer placed her
hand on her father's arm and spoke to him. His
eyes gleamed; he understood her thirst for re-

venge. He nodded and stood aside. As he left, the hangings fell into place with a sibilant whisper.

Nefer confronted me, smiling faintly. I suppose she hoped I would plead for my life. Instead, I dropped to my knees on the elaborate carpet spread on the sand. Not from fear, but from sheer exhaustion. A strange tranquility welled up within me. I was able to gaze calmly at Nefer by the light of lamps whose flames guttered in the seething of the wind. I was beyond anger.

From a divan the impatient young woman snatched a dagger. She pushed my head back and laid its cold edge against my throat. She said in Greek:

"For a long time I've wished for such a moment, harlot."

"I do not blame you, Queen Nefer."

"I intend to make your passing slow and painful, so you remember how you heaped insult upon me. Deny it, daughter of Herodias! Deny that you and your mother brought shame to a princess of Nabatea."

"I can't. It's the truth."

A scowl crossed her dark features.

"How is it that you bend so easily to my will?"

"I am weary. What is to be done will be done."

"Pretending to appease me won't save your life."

I raised my eyes to meet hers again, somehow no longer afraid.

"There is a higher will than yours or mine. If I die, I obey that will."

"But aren't you frightened? Such a young girl—once so finely dressed and well cared for—aren't you fearful to lose all that?"

"I lost it long ago. Whatever is to happen here has been willed to happen."

"It is *my* will—only mine—which rules this place! My will rules this knife, and this knife grants you death that is quick or death that is slow."

"No, Nefer. We are both powerless before that greater will."

"You've lost your senses."

"If so, it should have happened long ago."

"There is an odd brightness in your eyes—"

"Is there? Perhaps it's because I'm seeing the face of truth for the first time."

She held the blade close to my eyes. *"The truth is the edge of this knife!"*

I must have smiled. Nefer struck me and sent me sprawling. Her shoulders shook with rage.

"Grovel, Roman whore!"

"I can't."

"Cry for mercy! Entreat me to spare you!"

"Queen Nefer, I can't."

"You lie! This is all dissembling—trickery to stay my hand—"

"No. I am no longer afraid, and that is the truth. For a long time I've searched for strength, for some pattern in a world where everything seemed to be ugly and without a pattern. Finally the pattern's clear. The strength has flowed into me. You can take my life and I won't hate you. Your knife can bring darkness quickly or slowly, as you wish. I still won't hate you. You were wronged. It was I who wronged you, just as I wronged so many others. My father. The Essene—"

"Stop your babbling!" she cried. "All the talk and gods of Rome can't help you now."

"I know. They are false gods. The real god is here."

"There is no one here but the two of us!" Nefer exclaimed, her eyes bright with fear for one moment. "Who is this god you're prattling about?"

"I don't know His rightful name, Queen Nefer."

Her mouth curled with contempt.

"Then how do you know he exists?"

"Because I saw Him walking among men. I heard Him speak."

"Where did this happen? While you were cowering at the oasis?"

"Laugh at me if you will. You can't change what I feel in my heart."

Once more puzzlement showed itself in her eyes. Her hand trembled a little as she held the dagger close to my throat.

"I *order* you to tell me where you had this visitation from your god!"

"It was not a visitation. He walked among men in the body of a Jewish carpenter named Jesus of Nazareth."

"In the lands of Antipas?"

"That is where He may be found now. But a part of Him came here with me. Please, Queen Nefer, don't ask me to explain further. Anything I say will only anger you. But if you saw His face, you would understand. If you heard Him speak, you would believe."

Suddenly Nefer's shoulders began to tremble again, setting the bangles on her arms to rattling.

I bowed my head and held my hands together in the lap of my gown. I knew her anger would bring the final stroke, but my calm didn't weaken, nor my strength diminish.

I heard a soft thud. I looked up.

Nefer's hand was empty.

"I'm accursed," she breathed. Her fists drummed at her sides. "May I be damned for a weakling. May I burn in the seven hells for eternity. Stand up, Salome! Take yourself out of my sight!"

In astonishment, I stumbled to my feet. "Queen Nefer—"

She turned upon me, her eyes filled with an awful fear.

"I saw your god. I *saw* him!"

"But He is not here in the flesh to—"

"I saw Him on your *face!* I can't strike you because I dare not strike him. Whatever miracle he has worked in your soul has saved your life."

She flung out one hand.

"Go. Back to your people—but take your abominable god with you. He has made me afraid, and I am ashamed of my fear."

"Perhaps he is your god as well, Queen Nefer, though you call him by a different—"

"Go!" Tears of shame and anger coursed down her cheeks. "In a moment I might change my mind."

I walked to the pavilion entrance. When I pushed the hangings aside, I expected to find the desert men ready to carry out the execution Nefer had been unable to perform. Instead, I came face to face with Aretas.

His bearded face expressed astonishment. So

too did the faces of the Nabateans who opened a lane for me. I started to walk from the camp. My legs threatened to give way, but I tried not to show it. Though I might have craved death when Nefer bared her dagger, now I had to live. The God I had found had shown His face to Nefer, and that was a miracle too great to be destroyed.

With every step I took my courage mounted. I walked over the dune into the full fury of the storm. I had reached the end of my search.

Descending to the oasis, I walked slowly through the black ruins of the Roman chariots.

The trees had crashed over like pillars. Long palls of smoke drifted away toward the west. I could see the baggage wagons already loading for a retreat.

I stopped at the spot where I had left Marcus; a tree had fallen there. I knelt and dug beneath it. The sand was still hot.

There was no sign of him anywhere.

So the Nabateans had found and killed him. I only prayed his end had been easy.

Turning, I walked on to the Roman camp.

As I walked, I thought of my beloved. He had suffered great pain for my sake. An aching emptiness filled me again.

Seeing me approach, a Roman soldier ran to inform my mother. Through the swirling storm I saw Herodias rise up on one of the wagons and shield her eyes as she awaited my coming.

I walked on, ignoring the stares and whispers of the wounded soldiers straggling out behind the wagons.

As I walked to surrender to my mother, I spoke so that only one could hear.

"Not my will, but Thine. Not my will, but Thine."

Chapter IX

Damned

There was little difficulty on the return journey, save for constant sandstorms and inevitable hunger and thirst. But no second attack was mounted against us.

Why this was so, I could not tell. Perhaps it was due to the sudden change in Nefer's mood; perhaps to the fact that while Antipas had set out to show his strength to the Nabateans, he had been shown his weakness instead, and the single demonstration was sufficient for the time being.

In Fortress Machaerus the walls of loneliness closed about me once more.

I had sworn a vow to remain at my mother's side and would have carried it out willingly, had she bidden me to do so. She did not. After the limping retreat of the little army back across the Arnon, there were far too many things occupying her attention. I spent most of my time alone. I did not mind. I was content to meditate upon the words of the Nazarene, constantly finding new meanings and significance in them, as though they were jewels which might be polished and then polished again, revealing their beauty and luster more fully each time.

King Aretas was not content to sit passively by, however. Having found his enemy's strength wanting, he mounted a full-scale attack several weeks after our return. Legions were rushed to the frontiers. Border defenses were reported to be crumbling under the onslaught of a horde of the desert men.

Since Antipas' soldiers did not care for him, thinking him a fool and the plaything of my mother, they fared poorly in battle. When Antipas made his reports to the Emperor, disguise the facts with clever language though he might, the wily Sejanus at once saw the seriousness of the situation. Messages began to arrive almost daily, each one chastising Antipas more severely than the one before. I had no doubt that Pontius Pilate in Jerusalem was sending his own couriers to Capri with his own version of events, since several units under his command had also been rushed to the frontiers by direct order of Sejanus.

From the north came word that the Nazarene walked and spoke with new boldness, followed everywhere by hundreds of eager listeners. With all his resources employed eastward in the desert, Antipas could not quell this rising public sentiment. As a result, the name Jesus rapidly became a household word, even among the Roman slaves in the fortress who knew little of his teachings.

Worst of all was the madness of Antipas himself.

Night after night he ran screaming along the battlements above the sulphurous sea. The few soldiers left to defend the fortress told how he saw gory phantoms in the dark and fled from ghostly heads that dripped with blood—heads which he alone saw.

Once, in Rome, I had seen such a vision. It had been a portent of the strange, terrible road I was to follow to my lonely room in Machaerus. There, I felt certain I would end my days, perhaps slain by the Jews when they rose behind their leader Jesus to overthrow their conquerors. A peace of spirit had descended on me, a peace which made bearable the fulfillment of my vow to my mother.

But I would never find the complete serenity. The death of Marcus had left a void too great to be filled.

Yet I survived, friendless and gladly isolated from the wild revels held more and more frequently in the great hall. At first most of the detachment guarding Machaerus was invited. Soon all but the hardiest sickened of the ugly drunkenness into which Antipas descended in order to dull his sense of failure. A frightened slave girl told me the most dreadful debaucheries were practiced openly. Even my mother took part.

So as dark days settled upon Machaerus, I was

surprised to waken one morning to learn that a messenger from Philip the Tetrarch waited upon me.

I met him in the fortress garden. He was a polite, educated young Jew, a scribe and savant who served the old man. He went by the name Reuven. His message was simple.

"The tetrarch has sent me to ask that you reconsider his offer of marriage. He had thought you lost in the Nabatean wilderness, and was overjoyed when he learned you were alive. Now that a sufficient interval has passed since your return, he begs you to think again about your decision."

"Is the tetrarch well?" I asked.

A shadow crossed Reuven's dark eyes. "No. He is growing more feeble daily. He talks of no one but you. He's been very kind to me. He gave me an education worthy of a Roman youth. I can't help but speak in his behalf and urge you to accept."

"Reuven, I don't love the tetrarch. He is a kind man—but I don't love him."

"If that's all to stop you—I beg your pardon, Lady. He knows your feelings. He respects them. Still, he cherishes you. He will make no demands upon you except that you stay near him during his last days. He would be a good husband to you."

"There would be one other obstacle," I said, wavering a little. "I made a vow to stay with my mother."

Reuven couldn't control his smile. "Philip has already written her. She has consented."

I tried to mask my astonishment.

A moment later I realized I need not be a prisoner any longer.

"Very well." Slowly I drew a breath. "I will marry Philip whenever he wishes."

Reuven was overjoyed. "Thank you, Mistress. You are kind, generous—"

I shook my head. "No, Reuven. Only very lonely."

When he had gone, smiling and promising to send a splendid retinue to bring me to Bethsaida, I went in search of my mother.

I found her in the great hall. It was haunted with shadows in spite of the midday heat. The sight of Herodias bemused with wine, hair tangled, the kohl upon her eyes smeared, made me feel a compassion for her I had never known before.

She held out a trembling hand to grasp mine. Her touch was clammy. From the tower came a faint demented shriek. As it dwindled away, Herodias shuddered and closed her eyes.

"That is Antipas. There is nothing of the man I fell in love—"

"You fell in love with a dream, Mother. The crown of the Herods."

Wearily she shook her head. "I need no lectures on where I went astray. The fault is not with the ambition, but with its vessel. Antipas is weak—"

"I'm sorry. I did not mean to preach."

As though she had not even heard me she went on:

"—and already the dream is falling to pieces. Perhaps I could go to Jerusalem. Pilate is a clever man. Strong, too. He seems happily married. And yet—"

I shuddered at her crafty expression.

"Mother, I spoke with the scribe Reuven a moment ago."

"Did you give him an answer?"

"Yes. I will marry the tetrarch."

She sighed. "I'm glad. The terms of the marriage contract were very attractive. With what Philip is paying in exchange—Antipas has no treasure left with which to dower you—we can hire mercenary troops. Perhaps hold Aretas back until I can persuade Sejanus to send reinforcements. I may be forced to go to Capri to get it done. Yes, that mightn't be a bad idea. I'll go as soon as the Mare Nostrum calms, and I'm sure—"

"Mother."

"What?"

"Was the marriage arranged only to serve your ends?"

A bitter smile. "You know better than that. Any attempt to save Antipas is only temporary."

"Then why—?"

"Because—"

Her eyes softened a moment. I saw on her face a rare flash of affection—which might once have spared us both much misery.

"Because, Salome, every once in a while your mother recalls that she is a woman. There is another reason, too. You've changed. You're not the same girl I brought from Rome. Not even the same girl who danced before Antipas the night I trapped you into asking for the Essene's head. That girl—"

Herodias shrugged.

"Where has she gone? Died, perhaps? I'm not sure. I only know I was never uncertain of you

266

before. Never frightened. Now there's a new strength—a new calm about you. I don't understand it, but—"

I nodded. "That's why I can marry Philip."

Herodias leaped up, as though something had burst within her. She spoke in a voice I had never heard before—hoarse and oddly tender:

"Then hurry. Take slaves. Go alone to Bethsaida. Don't wait for Philip's retinue. But remember when you go that I have only one request. That you don't hate me to the end of your days."

"There is no hate in me, Mother."

She took a slow drink from her wine cup.

"I know. That's why I have to let you go." The old, lustful gleam returned. "It would never do for a mother to live with a daughter she couldn't control. Hurry, now. Don't waste a moment. You can be on the road before nightfall. I'll force Antipas to give you a guard."

"That won't be necessary. I'll wait for the retinue."

"No! I insist—one last time."

Another of those melancholy shrieks ghosted down to us, as though Antipas were crying to nameless gods for succor.

"By nightfall, Salome—before this place claims you forever." she turned away, her tone more harsh. "Besides, you'll only get in the way if you remain. I must make plans for the journey to Capri. If my mission fails, I'll be going directly to Jerusalem, and you'd only be a burden." She flung out a hand. "Be off."

I turned and left from the hall, wanting to hold her in my arms one last time but knowing she would never allow it. In the brief moments we

267

had faced one another, I had seen one more of the Nazarene's miracles. She had sent me to the tetrarch not only because she deemed it expedient, but because, in her own twisted fashion, she still loved me. She wanted me out of Machaerus because those who remained there were lost and damned.

The momentary revelation of her love, clumsy and awkward though it was, was a victory of sorts.

As she instructed, I set out on the road before sundown. I had my last glimpse of her standing alone on the ramparts of Machaerus, a small black figure against the immense scarlet sky.

She would never bow to her failure. She would wait until it destroyed her. I did not want to be present when that day came, and I think she did not want me to see the destruction.

She raised her hand briefly in salute. Then a towering rock hid her from view.

Chapter X

Bride of the Tetrarch

Because of the guard, we made the journey to Bethsaida unmolested.

On my first day there I did not see Philip. I was shown to my chambers, pleasant, airy rooms overlooking a garden rich with the fragrances of orange and pomegranate. Philip's servants did their best to look after my wants. When I was informed next evening that my future husband awaited me in the garden, I had lost some of the dejection I had felt on first entering his house and realizing I was about to become the wife of a dying man.

I chided myself for such ingratitude. Still, I couldn't quite throw off a feeling of gloom as I descended the outer stairs and moved among the trees in the first starlight.

Lamps gleamed at the windows. There was a breeze like a soft balm. A shadow stirred on a marble bench.

"I will repay you forever for the boon of this day," said Philip out of the darkness.

"I greet the Tetrarch. I thank him for making me welcome in his house."

"Come, Salome. Take a place beside me. I have something to show you."

He shifted about, hunting in the folds of his garments. At last he extended his hand, palm upward. There was a fragile smile on his face.

At once I felt my previous doubts washed away. By making his final days pleasant and comfortable, I could put to practice the shining lesson I had learned from Jesus. With a sense of purpose greater than any I had ever known, I sat down to see what it was he held in his hand. The object excited him to a state of almost boyish enthusiasm.

"Take it, Salome. Study it."

I did so. "It seems to be a coin. But it's unfamiliar."

"This is my wedding gift to you. Turn it so the light from the upper room falls over it. I'll admit it seems a paltry gift at first—there will be many more. But I thought it important to have this medallion cast."

"There's a man's face on it. Who is he?"

"Before I answer that, I must talk a little. This is the way we shall spend our wedding night—as well—sitting in the garden until weariness claims you."

"Tetrarch, my duty as a wife—"

He shook his head. "I am a sick man. My personal physician does all he can, but it is hopeless. In a year, a little more or a little less, these lands, for what they're worth, will be yours."

"Don't speak so, Tetrarch."

"Only a foolish man hides from the inevitable. The wise man accepts the fate of the gods, and makes his peace. I have made mine. I am prepared to spend the happiest year I have ever known on earth."

Tenderness overcame me. "I'll try to fill that time with as much joy as it will hold."

He smiled again. "I'd hoped you would accept the marriage proposal, not only because I'm a rather selfish old man who doesn't want to die alone, but also because I believe I can make you happy."

"Your kindness has done so already."

"That isn't what I mean. You once told someone—where and when escapes me—you told him I was a man who would help another if asked. The man you told wakened in the desert, nearly out of his mind with pain, feeling unbearable heat upon his body, seeing alien faces all around. He cried out, and strange men dragged him to their camp."

I sat rigid, wondering whether his mind had suddenly taken the cruel path of senility. Was he bent on tormenting me? It seemed impossible, yet I had no other explanation.

"The desert people are skilled in the healing arts," he went on. "Theirs is a culture far older than that of Rome. This man I mentioned was restored to life. He spoke the name of a certain woman and was promptly given his freedom by a desert princess. Such a generous act astonished him. Why should a sworn enemy set him free? But he didn't question the miracle. Instead he came here, seeking refuge from the Romans who would arrest him for being an escaped slave."

"Tetrarch, you can't be speaking of anyone but Marcus Catullus. He's dead."

"Look closely at the medallion."

"I did. The profile is strangely familiar. But the cheekbones, the eye sockets—perhaps it's the light. I've never seen this man before."

"The likeness was cast by an artisan on my estates outside the city, in return for service by my personal physician. He saved the artisan's son from death. The physician's name is Aristobalus. You are looking at the side of his face that was torn away by a Roman whip—and restored by the healing arts of the Nabateans."

Once more I held the medallion to the light. For the first time I saw that the face was so exquisitely cast that the very scars on the stranger's face stood out in bold relief.

"Is it really Marcus? Is he alive?"

"That is my personal physician, Aristobalus. Marcus is dead."

"Tetrarch—"

"Let me speak, child. As my wife, you will be safe from your family. In my household, with a new face and a new name, he is safe from the authority of Rome. He doesn't know you're here, or even that you are to marry me. I deemed it wiser to send him to my outlying lands for a time. I'll call for him when I have need of him—within the year, I'm sure. After a suitable mourning, you may claim this wedding gift I give you for your comfort and nearness."

So saying, he slipped the medallion into my hand and closed my fingers around it.

My heart trembled within my breast as I marveled at the miracle of love he had unfolded before me. Then I remembered that I owed him a duty. I touched his arm.

"Don't be afraid to kiss me, Tetrarch. Tomorrow I'll be your wife."

Smiling, he shook his head. Almost shyly he slipped his arm around my shoulders.

"An old man has no need of the kisses of the young. But the young have warmth—and I am cold, even though the night is balmy. It's a comfort just to sit beside you. Look at the stars, child. They're beautiful in this part of the world. Long ago they taught me that there is beauty if you but raise your eyes—and that moments like this make all of life's pain worthwhile."

He lapsed into silence. My heart welled with happiness. I took his hand between mine while the night darkened around us and the stars came out in all their splendor.

With publication in January, 1976, of the fourth volume of The American Bicentennial Series, John Jakes became the first author in history to have three novels on national best-seller lists within a single year ... climaxing a twenty-five-year professional writing career which began with sale of a science fiction short story (for $25) to *The Magazine of Fantasy and Science Fiction* in 1951. A native of Chicago and still a Midwestern resident, Jakes sold his first story while in his second year of college, and his first book—an historical Western for young people—twelve months later. Since then he has published more than fifty books and two hundred short pieces ranging from science fiction to suspense, and fiction and nonfiction for young people, including a biography of the Mohawk chief, Joseph Brant, and a history of the TIROS weather satellite program. Most of this work was produced while Jakes held creative posts with advertising agencies, working on behalf of some of America's largest companies; he left advertising in 1970 to write full time. He remains an avid community theater actor and playwright (eleven of his plays and musicals have been published), as well as a lifelong history buff. His interest in history led to half a dozen historical novels—originally written under his "Jay Scotland" pseudonym—which Pinnacle Books is now publishing in completely revised, uniform editions.

Pinnacle Books proudly presents

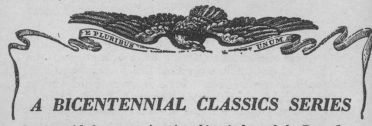

A BICENTENNIAL CLASSICS SERIES

Starting with four great American historical novels by Bruce Lancaster, one of America's most distinguished historians.

———TRUMPET TO ARMS An exceptionally crafted romance spun beautifully amidst the fury of the American Revolution. (PB-887, 1.75)
"Explosive in style . . . *Trumpet to Arms* is always easy to read and strikes a note as stirring as a call to battle."
—The Boston Globe

———THE SECRET ROAD A fascinating, yet little known account of the exploits of Washington's Secret Service. A gripping story of America's first espionage unit. (PB-889, 1.75)
"A veteran craftsman at the top of his form."
—The New York Times

———PHANTOM FORTRESS A masterful treatment of the career of General Francis Marion, known to history as "The Swamp Fox." (PB-905, 1.75)
"History that is good and galloping, for competent scholarship underlies the romantic story."
—New York Herald Tribune

———BLIND JOURNEY An absorbing tale of romance and adventure that moves from 18th-century France and its grandeur to the carnage of revolutionary America. A story no one should miss. (PB-915, 1.75)
"Romance, adventure . . . full pulsing life. Bruce Lancaster's best."
—The Boston Herald

Check which books you want. If you can't find any of these books at your local bookstore, simply send the cover price plus 25¢ per book for postage and handling to us and we'll mail you your book(s).

PINNACLE BOOKS
275 Madison Avenue, New York, New York 10016

A Question of Balance—
perhaps the most important question the United States will ever answer—perhaps the last.

?

⊚

Conflict between Russia and China is inevitable—
What does the United States do when *both* sides come for help?

This is

THE CHINESE ULTIMATUM

P974 $1.95

The year is 1977. Russia and China have assembled troops on the Mongolian border, and are fighting a "limited" war. A reunited Germany and a bellicose Japanese military state have joined the battle. The United States must step in, or be considered the enemies of both. The Chinese have said their last word on the subject—what will ours be?

"Absolutely gripping, I couldn't put it down."
　　　　　　　—Rowland Evans, syndicated political columnist
"This novel is too incredibly real . . . and damnably possible!"
　　　　　　　—an anonymous State Department official

ARE YOU A LATE MOVIE FAN . . .
OR A DYED-IN-THE-WOOL
HOLLYWOOD BUFF? If so, here
are some stories of the stars
that will keep you up even later!

_____THE CURIOUS DEATH OF MARILYN MONROE
by Robert F. Slatzer   P573 $1.95

_____THE JAMES DEAN STORY by Ron Martinetti
P633 $1.50

_____SINATRA by Tony Sciacca   P847 $1.75

_____SOPHIA: An intimate biography by Donald Zec
P863 $1.75

_____KING OF COMEDY by Mack Sennett
P652 $1.75

_____SUSAN HAYWARD: Her Complete Life Story by
Doug McClelland   P706 $1.50

_____WOODY ALLEN: The Clown Prince of American
Humor by Bill Adler & Jeffrey Feinman
P786 $1.75

_____BRONSON! by W. R. Harbinson   P696 $1.50

_____THOSE WILD, WILD KENNEDY BOYS by Peter
Brennan & Stephen Dunleavy   P968 $1.75

_____THE WISDOM OF BRUCE LEE by Felix Dennis &
Roger Hutchinson   P862 $1.75

If you are unable to find any of these titles at your
local bookstore, simply send the cover price, plus
25¢ for postage and handling to:

PINNACLE BOOKS, 275 Madison Avenue,
New York, N.Y. 10016